Jordan stared at him. "Xavier?" Her voice emerged as a breathless whisper. "Wh-what are you doing?"

"Making a point," he rasped.

And then his mouth came down on hers and Jordan felt as if she'd slammed into a wall of electricity, shock and heat consuming her so completely she could do nothing more than tremble and burn under the savagery of his kiss.

And it *was* savage. Like no other kiss she'd ever experienced before. A kiss of anger and dominance and control. It should have horrified her, incensed her, but there was something sinfully sensual, darkly exhilarating, about the way his firm lips moved with such brutal purpose over hers.

She made a sound she told herself was protest but knew was actually acquiescence. Heat stung her body in places he wasn't even touching. And where he did touch...she felt branded. *Claimed.* By his hands. His mouth. Even the scrape of his thick stubble on her skin seemed like a deliberate attempt to mark and punish.

Never in her life had she been kissed with such utter, breathtaking mastery.

Ruthless Billionaire Brothers

*These brothers have conquered everything—
except love!*

The de la Vega brothers may not be bonded by
blood, but these billionaires are united by their
legendary business success! Neither has failed in
the acquisition of wealth and power. But they're
both about to realize there might be one thing just
beyond their reach...

Two irresistible women are about to interfere in
their well-laid plans—and the sparks that fly will
result in burning seduction!

Read Ramon and Emily's story in
A Night, A Consequence, A Vow

And read Xavier and Jordan's story in
A Mistress, A Scandal, A Ring

Both available now!

Angela Bissell

A MISTRESS, A SCANDAL, A RING

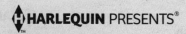

Recycling programs
for this product may
not exist in your area.

ISBN-13: 978-1-335-41955-2

A Mistress, A Scandal, A Ring

First North American publication 2018

Copyright © 2018 by Angela Bissell

Printed in U.S.A.

www.Harlequin.com

Angela Bissell lives with her husband and one crazy ragdoll cat in the vibrant harborside city of Wellington, New Zealand. In her twenties, with a wad of savings and a few meager possessions, she took off for Europe, backpacking through Egypt, Israel, Turkey and the Greek Islands before finding her way to London, where she settled and worked in a glamorous hotel for several years. Clearly the perfect grounding for her love of Harlequin Presents! Visit her at angelabissell.com.

Books by Angela Bissell

Harlequin Presents

Ruthless Billionaire Brothers

A Night, A Consequence, A Vow

Irresistible Mediterranean Tycoons

Surrendering to the Vengeful Italian
Defying Her Billionaire Protector

Visit the Author Profile page
at Harlequin.com for more titles.

This book is dedicated to the memory of Susan Chapman, aka Lily Shepherd, an amazing lady who faced her final days with strength, grace and tremendous courage. She will be sadly missed and fondly remembered by her friends in the romance writing community.

CHAPTER ONE

'YOU MUST LEAVE NOW, *senyorita.*'

Jordan Walsh tipped her head back, and back some more, until she stared into the face of the uniformed security guard who towered over her.

'I'm not leaving,' she told him, making no move to vacate the chair she had occupied for over two hours in the waiting area of this vast marble foyer.

The big man's eyebrows beetled together. 'You must go. The building is closing.'

The building was the Vega Tower—a great big steel and glass monolith that rose from the heart of Barcelona's thriving business district and dwarfed everything around it. It had cost one point two billion US dollars to construct, had taken two years and three months from foundation to completion, and comprised forty-four floors of bustling head office activity for one of Europe's largest and most successful multinational conglomerates.

Jordan was well acquainted with these facts because she had picked up the glossy hardbound book titled *The Vega Corporation: Sixty Years of Success* off the low table beside her and, out of sheer boredom, read the entire thing from front cover to back. Twice.

'I'm not leaving without an appointment to see Mr de la Vega,' she said.

This was not news to the security man. She had made the same request on her arrival, and again an hour ago when it had become obvious that his call to the CEO's assistant had garnered no result.

'He is not available.'

'Which is why I want to make an appointment,' she explained with exaggerated patience. 'So that I can see him when he *is* available.'

'It is not possible,' the man said, and with that he clamped a giant hand around her upper arm and hauled her to her feet.

Jordan gasped. 'Wait!' She braced her legs to resist, her flat rubber-soled shoes giving her feet a much-needed moment of purchase on the shiny marble. 'You're not seriously going to manhandle me out of the building?'

'I am sorry, *senyorita*,' he said, but the sidelong glance he sent her didn't look apologetic so much as… pitying.

She bristled at the implication of that look. It wasn't difficult to guess what he and his colleagues behind the desk were thinking. A man as wealthy and powerful as their boss must have an abundance of female admirers and hangers-on, and his staff were no doubt required to act as gatekeepers on occasion.

But Jordan was no jilted lover or wannabe mistress. 'Please,' she persisted, hating the desperate note that crept into her voice. 'Can you just call his office one more time?'

Somebody must still be up there. Sure, it was almost six-thirty p.m., but didn't working hours in Spain differ from the norm at home? And hadn't she read an online article just yesterday in which the CEO was quoted as saying he not only worked long hours himself, but expected key members of his staff to do the same?

But the guard shook his head. 'Call tomorrow,' he said.

Jordan felt the sharp bite of frustration in her belly. She'd already phoned the day before, and the day before that. Each time she'd been stonewalled by the CEO's uppity assistant. Which was why she had trekked across the city in the stifling mid-August heat this afternoon and shown up in person.

She planted her feet and locked her knees, but her strength was no match for the guard's. He started walking and she was forced to stumble along beside him, clutching her tote bag and the shreds of her dignity as he marched her towards the automatic sliding glass doors.

Her heart lurched. A few more steps and she'd be out on the street, back to square one.

The glass doors parted before them, letting in a blast of hot air, and she thought of the envelope in her bag—the letter she'd carried ten thousand miles across the globe—and a crushing sense of failure engulfed her.

All because she couldn't find her way to the top of this imposing corporate fortress to see one man.

Her body stiffened in protest. 'I'm Mr de la Vega's stepsister!' she cried out, and the guard pulled up short, surprise making his grip slacken just enough so she could wrench herself free.

Around them the cavernous foyer came to a standstill, the other security personnel behind the desk and the few office workers making their way to and from the lifts having paused and fallen silent in the wake of her outburst.

A tidal wave of heat swept up her body and into her face. Doing her best to ignore the curious stares, she levelled her gaze at the guard and said quietly, 'I'm sure neither his assistant—nor you—would like to inform him that you've turned me away.'

The man rubbed the back of his neck, his face screwed up in a grimace of indecision. Finally, he said in a gruff voice, 'Please wait.'

He returned to the desk to make a phone call and two minutes later a tall, elegant woman wearing a sleek navy shift dress and high heels emerged from a lift. She looked to the guard, who steered her in Jordan's direction with a tilt of his head.

Jordan saw the woman give her an assessing, narrow-eyed once-over before striding across the marble floor towards her.

'Ms Walsh.' Her tone was cool. 'Mr de la Vega is extremely busy, but he is willing to give you ten minutes of his time.'

Her English was accented, but good, and Jordan recognised the voice at once. She was the assistant who'd screened her phone calls and refused to give her an appointment.

Jordan forced a smile and resisted asking if Mr de la Vega was sure he could spare a *whole* ten minutes from his extremely busy schedule. Instead she offered a gracious, 'Thank you,' but the woman had already pivoted on a spiked heel and started back across the foyer, leaving Jordan to follow.

The guard held the lift doors open and then boarded

with them, taking a position at the rear as they hurtled upwards to the forty-fourth floor.

Jordan's heart raced and her hands grew clammy. After all the careful thought she'd put into this, the endless days of agonising indecision, the time spent working out what she'd say when...*if*...this moment came, she hadn't expected to feel quite so nervous.

But then it was no small thing she was about to do. She had no idea how Xavier de la Vega would receive her. How he'd react. She wasn't sure how she'd react herself in his position.

She cast a critical glance at her reflection in the highly polished panels of the lift doors. In a sleeveless white blouse, khaki capris and a pair of comfy shoes, she looked plain and unremarkable next to the tall, stunning Spanish woman. Her one feature worthy of note—her long, copper-red hair—was pulled into a high, no-fuss ponytail, and the tinted moisturiser she'd rubbed into her skin that morning was the closest thing to make-up her face had seen in weeks.

The lift doors opened and all thoughts of her appearance were swiftly forgotten as she followed the other woman into a large suite of offices. They walked along a wide corridor and she was conscious of the guard trailing close behind them, of thick carpet underfoot, high walls hung with expensive artwork and a hushed atmosphere. But the escalating flutter of nerves in her belly made everything else a blur.

And then they entered a big corner office and every shred of her attention was snagged and held by the man sitting behind the massive oak desk.

Jordan had seen photos of him online. Not many, mind you. Unlike his younger brother, of whom there were literally hundreds of photos scattered across the Internet, Xavier de la Vega appeared to value his privacy. But as her breath caught and her hands inexplicably shook she realised those two-dimensional images had not in any way prepared her for a personal, up-close encounter with this devastatingly handsome man.

And his eyes.

Grey…just like Camila's.

Her throat thickened and she had to swallow hard and blink fast to contain her emotion.

He stood, and she was struck by his height. Six foot at least, which surprised her. Her stepmother had been tiny, her figure perfectly proportioned but petite. By the time Jordan had turned sixteen she'd easily been able to rest her chin on top of Camila's head when they'd hugged.

He walked around the desk and she saw that everything about him, from his neatly cropped black hair to his tailored grey suit and expensive-looking leather shoes, was immaculate. Even the full Windsor knot in his tie looked as if it had been flawlessly executed.

He had an air of authority about him—and something else she couldn't quite pinpoint.

Arrogance?

Impatience?

Her gaze went to the hard line of his jaw and then up to his high, intelligent forehead and slashing jet-black eyebrows.

Yes, she concluded with a touch of unease. This man looked as if he had little tolerance for weakness or compromise.

Suddenly she was conscious of the silence blanketing the room. Of the fact that he was returning her scrutiny with hard, narrowed eyes. He didn't smile. He didn't even step forward and offer to shake her hand in greeting. Which probably wasn't a bad thing, given her hands now felt as damp as soggy dishrags.

His attention shifted to his assistant. '*Gràcies*, Lucia,' he said, his voice deep and rich and undeniably masculine. 'Leave us, please.'

He looked to the guard and said something in Spanish—or perhaps he spoke in Catalan, since she'd read that he spoke both languages fluently, along with English and French—and she tried to pretend her knees hadn't just gone a little weak. She loved the romance languages, and despite his forbidding demeanour there was something indescribably sexy about the way Xavier de la Vega spoke in his native tongue.

The guard responded, but whatever he said it only drew a terse, dismissive word from his boss, and he quickly joined Lucia in vacating the room, closing the door on his way out.

Those grey eyes—a shade or two darker than Camila's, she realised now—settled on her again.

'My staff are concerned for my safety.'

It wasn't the start to their conversation she'd anticipated. She blinked, confused. 'Why?'

'They believe you might pose a threat,' he elaborated, watching her closely. 'Do you, Ms Walsh?'

Her eyes widened. 'A physical threat, you mean?' The notion was so preposterous a little laugh bubbled up her throat. 'Hardly.'

'Indeed.' His tone and the way his gaze raked over her, as though assessing her physical capabilities, implied that he too considered the idea ludicrous. 'Are you a journalist?' he asked abruptly.

'No,' she said, trying to ignore the disconcerting pulse of heat that fired through her body in the wake of his cursory appraisal. 'Why would you think that?'

His penetrating gaze locked onto hers. 'Journalists have a tendency to get creative in their attempts to access whomever they're pursuing.'

She frowned. 'I'm afraid I don't follow.'

'You claim to be my stepsister.'

'Ah…' She felt her cheeks grow pink. 'I can explain that…'

'Can you, Ms Walsh?' His tone was hard. 'Because the last time I checked my parents were still happily married—to each other. To my knowledge, neither of them is hiding additional spouses or secret stepchildren.'

Her blush intensified. She had expected this to be tricky. It was why she'd put such careful thought into what she would say and how she'd say it if she ever got the chance. But now that she was here and he was standing before her, so much more imposing in the flesh than she'd imagined, she couldn't recall a single one of the sentences she'd so painstakingly crafted in her mind.

She swallowed. 'Um… Maybe we could sit down?' she suggested.

For a long moment he didn't move, just stood there staring at her, eyes narrowed to slits of silver-grey as if he were debating whether to have her thrown out or let her stay. Finally, just as her composure teetered on the brink of collapse, he gestured to a chair in front of his desk.

Relief pushed a smile onto her face. 'Thank you,' she said, and noted that he waited until she was seated before sitting in his own chair.

It was a simple, old-fashioned courtesy that made her warm to him a bit—until he opened his mouth again.

'Start talking, Ms Walsh. I don't have all evening.'

The smile evaporated from her face. *Good grief.* Was he this brusque with everyone? Or only with strangers who dared to ask for a piece of his precious time?

She sat up a little straighter and said, 'Jordan.'

'Excuse me?'

'My first name is Jordan.'

He drummed the long, tapered fingers of his right hand on the top of the desk, then abruptly stopped, curling his hand into a loose fist. 'Your accent—is it Australian?'

'Yes. I'm from Melbourne.'

She paused, took a deep breath, then opened her tote bag and pulled out her red leather-bound journal. She undid the clasp and lifted the cover. The sealed envelope and the two photos she'd carefully tucked inside the journal were still there, safe and sound.

'Until recently I lived there with my stepmother.' She picked up one of the photos and held it out, her arm extended across the desk. 'Camila Walsh.'

He glanced at the photo, but no flicker of recognition showed on his face. Jordan didn't know why that should disappoint her. Of course he wouldn't recognise her stepmother.

But her eyes…

Could he not see they were *his* eyes?

'Her maiden name was Sanchez,' she added. 'She was originally from a small village north of here.'

'Was?'

A stillness had come over him and Jordan hesitated, all the doubts she'd thought she'd laid to rest suddenly rearing up again, pushing at the walls of her resolve. For the past ten days she'd ridden a wave of certainty, firm in her belief that what she was doing was not only the right thing but a *good* thing.

After weeks of feeling lost and alone, adrift, with no job, nothing and no one left in the world to anchor her, she'd booked her flights to Spain almost with a sense of euphoria.

'She died six weeks ago.'

Somehow she managed to say the words without her voice wobbling. She lowered her arm and stared down at the photo of her stepmother.

'I am sorry for your loss.'

She looked up. The sentiment in his deep voice had sounded genuine. 'Thank you.'

Her gaze meshed with his and the intensity of those sharp, intelligent eyes made her breath catch in her throat. She shifted a bit, unsettled by her escalating awareness of him. He was so handsome. So compelling. She couldn't take her eyes off him. And that preternatural stillness in his body… It was disconcerting, making her think of the big, predatory cats in the wildlife documentaries her dad had loved to watch.

She took another deep breath, in through her nose, out through her mouth, the way Camila had taught her to do as a child to combat stress. He was waiting for her to speak—to spell out why she was here. Did he already have an inkling? She searched his face, but the chiselled features were impassive, giving nothing away.

Adopting the tone she often used at work when a mix of practicality and compassion was required, she said, 'Camila was your birth mother.'

The statement landed between them like a burning stick of dynamite tossed into the room. Jordan braced herself for its impact, her whole body tensing, but if Xavier de la Vega was even mildly shocked he hid it well.

'You have proof of this?'

She blinked at him. It was such a cool, controlled response—far less emotional than anything she'd expected—but she counselled herself not to read too much into it. At twenty-six years of age, and after five years of working as a trauma nurse, she'd seen people react in all kinds of ways in all sorts of life-altering situations. Often what showed on the surface belied the tumult within.

She slid the other photo from her journal across the desk to him. This one was older, its colours faded, the edges a little bit worn.

He leaned forward, gave the photo a cursory glance, then drew back. 'This tells me nothing,' he said dismissively.

Jordan withdrew her hand, leaving the photo on his desk. 'It's you,' she said, and it gave her heart a funny little jolt to think that the tiny, innocent baby in the photo had grown into the powerful, intimidating man before her.

His frown sharpened and he flicked his hand towards the photo, the gesture faintly disdainful. 'This child could be anyone.'

She reached forward and flipped the photo over. The blue ink on the back had faded with time, but Camila's handwriting was still legible. 'It says "Xavier",' she pointed out, and waited, sensing his reluctance to look again. When he did, she saw his eyes widen a fraction. 'And the date of birth underneath... I believe it's—'

'Mine,' he bit out, cutting her off before she could finish. He sat back, nostrils flaring, a white line of tension forming around his mouth. 'It is no secret that I am adopted. An old photo with my forename and my birth date written on it proves nothing.'

'Perhaps not,' she conceded, determined to hold her nerve in the face of his denial and the hostility she sensed was gathering in him. 'But my stepmother told me things. Details that only your adoptive parents or your birth mother could know.'

His eyes darkened, the grey irises no more than a glint of cold steel between the thick fringes of his ebony lashes. 'Such as?'

Her lips felt bone-dry all of a sudden, and she moistened them with her tongue. 'Thirty-five years ago Regina Martinez worked as a housekeeper for your parents,' she began, carefully reciting the details Camila had shared with her for the first time just a month before she had died. 'She had an eighteen-year-old unmarried niece who fell pregnant. At the time, your parents were considering adopting a child after your mother had had several miscarriages. A private adoption was arranged, and soon after you were born—at a private hospital here in Barcelona which your parents paid for—they took you home.'

And the young Camila had been devastated, even though she had done the only thing she could. The alternative—living as an unwed mother under her strict father's roof in their small, conservative village—would have heaped as much misery and shame on her child's life as on her own.

Knowing first-hand how it felt to be genuinely unwanted by one's biological mother, Jordan hoped Xavier would see Camila's decision not as an act of rejection or abandonment, but one of love.

She waited for him to say something. It was perfectly understandable that he might need a minute or two to process what she had told him. Something like this was—

'What do you want, Ms Walsh?'

Her thoughts slammed to a halt, the question—not to mention the distinct chill in his voice—taking her by surprise. 'Excuse me?'

'Money?'

She stared at him. 'Money?' she echoed blankly.

His gaze was piercing, the colour of his eyes the dark pewter of storm clouds under his lowered brows. 'It is common knowledge that my family is one of the wealthiest in Spain. You would not be the first to claim a tenuous connection in hopes of a hand-out.'

A hand-out? Her head snapped back as if he'd flung acid at her face. She gripped the edges of her journal, shock receding beneath a rush of indignation. 'That is offensive,' she choked out.

'Quite,' he agreed. 'Which is why I will ask you again—what do you want, Ms Walsh?'

Jordan felt her heart begin to pound. How on earth could this arrogant, imperious man be her stepmother's son?

Camila had been a kind, gentle soul, who'd always looked for the best in people despite the heartbreak she'd suffered early in her life.

Jordan looked at the envelope she'd placed with such reverent care between the pages of her journal. She'd carried the envelope halfway around the world and not once had she been tempted to snoop inside it. The letter it contained was private, sacred—the precious words of a dying woman to her son.

Lifting her chin, she looked him in the eye, letting him know he didn't intimidate her—that she had nothing to feel ashamed about. She held up the envelope. 'I came here to give you this.'

'And what is "this"?'

'A letter from your birth mother.'

'Camila Walsh?'

'Yes—your birth mother,' she reiterated.

A muscle worked in his jaw. His gaze flicked to the photo that lay face-down on his desk, then back to her. 'A claim which is, at present, unsubstantiated.'

Jordan let her hand fall back to her lap, her frustration so great she wanted to slap her palm against the top of his desk and demand to know why he was being so bloody-minded. Instead, she clamped her back teeth together and waited for the impulse to pass.

She was not someone who flew off the handle at the slightest provocation. She might have been saddled with her mother's unruly flame-coloured hair but she hadn't, thank goodness, inherited her fiery personality.

Suddenly she felt as cross with herself as she did with him. Why hadn't she been better prepared for this kind of reaction? Had she imagined that because she and Camila had been close she would automatically feel some sort of instant kinship with this man?

Sadly, she had. She'd tucked her grief away in a safely locked compartment of her heart, donned those silly rose-coloured glasses she should have learnt to distrust years ago, and set off on her mission to deliver Camila's letter and scatter her ashes in the homeland she'd left thirty-three years before.

It was the final thing Jordan would be able to do for her stepmom—for the woman whose love and kindness had helped to heal the wound Jordan's mother had inflicted years earlier with her abrupt, unapologetic departure from her daughter's life.

And, embarrassing though it was to admit it, Jordan *had* built up a little fantasy in her head—imagining herself striking up a friendship with Camila's son, having a kind of stepsibling relationship with him—which, now that she was here, seemed totally laughable.

This was not a man she could imagine having such a relationship with. Girls did not look at their brothers and feel their skin prickle and heat or their mouths go dry.

He wasn't even the sort of man she liked. In fact he was everything she *dis*liked. Arrogant. Superior. Unfeeling. A self-appointed demigod in a power suit, ruling his kingdom from the top of his gilded tower.

And Jordan knew all about men with god complexes, didn't she? She'd dated a surgeon whose ego was the size of the Sydney Opera House and then—even worse, because she should have known better—she'd moved in with him and decided she was in love.

Jamming the brakes on her runaway thoughts, she focused on the cold, handsome face of the man in front of her and made a snap decision. 'I don't think you're ready for this letter, Mr de la Vega.'

And in that moment she knew *she* wasn't ready to relinquish it—because what if he didn't treat it with the respect it deserved? What if he threw it away without even reading it?

Stiffening her resolve, she tucked the envelope into her journal, then tore out a blank page from the back, pulled a pen from her tote bag and scribbled down her mobile number. 'I'll be staying at the Hostel Jardí across town for a few more days and then I'm travelling to

Mallorca and then Madrid.' She put the piece of paper on his desk. 'If you want to reach me, here's my number.' She bundled her things back into her tote and slung the strap over her shoulder. 'Thank you for seeing me, Mr de la Vega.' And she turned to go.

'Ms Walsh.'

His deep, commanding voice brought her to a standstill and her heart leapt with hope. Had he had an epiphany? Realised, perhaps, that he'd behaved abominably?

Breath held, she turned back…and her heart landed with a heavy thud of disappointment.

He was standing, arm extended, holding out the photo she'd left on his desk—the one of himself as a baby. 'You forgot this.'

Releasing her breath, she shook her head. 'It's yours. Keep it—or throw it away. Up to you.'

She continued on to the door, and for a few agonising seconds her nerveless fingers fumbled with the handle while her nape prickled from the unsettling sensation of his gaze drilling into her back.

But he didn't call her name again. Didn't attempt to stop her.

As she walked past his assistant's desk and the stunning Lucia half rose out of her chair, Jordan held up her palm. 'I can see myself out, thanks.'

Her chest was so tight it wasn't until she stepped onto the street forty-four storeys below that she felt able to draw a full, oxygen-laden breath into her lungs again.

But as she set off across the city no amount of deep breathing could lift the weight from her heart.

Damn him.

What was she supposed to do now with her stepmom's letter?

CHAPTER TWO

'I'VE LOCATED THE PAPERWORK,' said Roberto Fuentes, long-time solicitor and a trusted friend to the de la Vega family for over forty years. He paused, and a ripple of disquiet ran beneath the surface of Xav's iron-clad self-control.

Xav rose from behind his desk, his mobile pressed tightly to his ear. Three short strides brought him to a thick wall of glass—one of two floor-to-ceiling panes that afforded his office in the Vega Tower a panoramic view of the sprawling, sun-baked metropolis below.

He stared blindly out at the cityscape, his body bristling with impatience under the impeccably tailored lines of his charcoal-grey suit. 'And?'

'Your birth mother's name was Camila Sanchez.'

The first cold prickles of shock needled over his scalp, even though the solicitor only confirmed what he already knew in his gut was true.

He raised his left arm and leant his palm against the window, needing to steady himself.

He didn't suffer from vertigo, or a fear of heights, but suddenly the sheer drop on the other side of the glass to the city street over forty storeys below induced a wave of dizziness.

'Xavier—?'

'I heard you, Roberto.' He backed away from the window and returned to his desk. 'Was she related to anyone in my parents' employ?'

Another heavy pause. 'With the greatest respect, Xavier... I really would feel more comfortable if you had this conversation with Elena and Vittorio. They've always said—'

'No.' He cut Roberto off. He knew what his parents had always said.

'We love you. Nothing will ever change that.'

And in thirty-five years nothing ever had. Not even the unexpected arrival of his younger brother, Ramon, the 'miracle baby' the doctors had told his mother she'd never have.

His parents had also told him that if one day he decided he wanted to trace his biological family they would support him in that quest. He'd never chosen that path, but he knew that if he had they would have stayed true to their word.

Because Vittorio and Elena de la Vega were good people. Good parents.

Xav had worked hard over the years to make them proud. Worked harder still to prove to those members of the extended family who'd never accepted him as one of their own that he was worthy of the de la Vega name.

As a boy, seeing how the veiled barbs and sly taunts upset his *mamá* had made him even more determined to prove he was just as good as, if not better than, any of *them*.

Years later, he still faced the same insidious prejudices—but now he had the pleasure of rubbing his detractors' noses in his unrivalled success.

No. Despite the solicitor's discomfort, Xav would not involve his parents at this point. He would shield them. Protect them. At least until he understood what—or rather *who*—he was dealing with.

He sat down at the handcrafted oak desk that had been handed down from father to son, along with the role of Chief Executive, through four generations of de la Vega menfolk over a span of more than sixty years.

'This conversation remains strictly between you and me,' he said. 'Are we clear?'

'As you wish,' the older man said, resigned but respectful. 'Just a moment…'

Xav heard the sounds of papers being shuffled before Roberto spoke again.

'Ah… I remember now. Miss Sanchez was the niece of your parents' housekeeper at the time. The adoption was private, the paperwork drawn up through this office.'

Xav was silent a moment, his mind processing. Assimilating. Finally, he said, '*Gràcies*, Roberto. I appreciate your help—and discretion,' he emphasised, and then he ended the call and immediately made another.

The security specialist the Vega Corporation kept on retainer answered on the first ring. 'I just emailed the dossier through to you,' the man said without preamble.

'Any red flags?'

'None. A couple of parking offences, but nothing more serious. She's single, a qualified trauma nurse currently unemployed. Presence on social media is sporadic and low-key. Mother lives in North America. Father's dead—and, yes, he was married to a Camila Walsh, nee Sanchez, now also deceased.' He paused. 'Without knowing what your specific concerns are, I'd say she's pretty harmless.'

Xav twisted his lips. Any man who believed women were harmless was a fool. He knew from experience they weren't. It was why he'd taken exceptional care in choosing his lovers over the last decade—and why he was being equally judicious in choosing a wife.

'And the surveillance?' he asked.

'We've still got eyes on her. She was at a dance club till one a.m. She hasn't left the hostel yet this morning.'

Xav narrowed his eyes. Jordan Walsh was an unemployed *party girl*? 'Keep me apprised of her movements.' He tapped his keyboard to bring his computer screen to life. 'I'll let you know if I need anything further.'

He put his phone down, located the email in his inbox and opened the attachment. The first section of the document covered basic stats—name, age, marital status, occupation—and included a photo: a full-colour head-and-shoulders shot that had probably come from one of her social media accounts. She was smiling into the camera lens, giving the illusion that she was smiling straight at him, and just looking at the image gave him the same visceral gut-punch reaction that he'd experienced last night when she'd walked into his office.

Right before she had turned his world on its head and then stalked out.

Over the years he'd met hundreds of beautiful women, had slept with a select few, but never had he been so immediately or powerfully arrested by a woman's looks before.

Her colouring was striking, with a head-turning combination of Titian hair and extraordinary hazel eyes which were a fascinating blend of green and gold. Her features were strong and symmetrical, with bold cheekbones, a straight nose and a wide, generous mouth.

Not pretty by conventional standards, perhaps, but stunning nevertheless.

Abruptly he sat back, irritated at his unusual lack of focus. Jordan Walsh's looks, however remarkable, were irrelevant. She was a problem to be handled—that was all. One he needed to contain until he understood what threat, if any, she posed. Just as his feelings about his birth mother would have to be shelved and examined at a later stage. He didn't have time for distractions. He had a global corporation to run. A multimillion-dollar acquisition to negotiate—a major deal that at least one member of the board would relish seeing him fail to close.

He opened the drawer where he'd shoved the photo and the piece of paper she'd left on his desk last night. He picked up his phone to punch in the number she'd written down, but then suddenly changed his mind, slipped the paper and his phone into his jacket pocket and stood.

In the anteroom outside his office he paused by Lucia's desk and checked his watch. It was ten-twenty a.m. 'I'm heading out,' he told her.

Her heavily made-up eyes blinked as if he'd said something unintelligible. She glanced at her computer screen. 'But…you have a ten-thirty meeting with the Marketing Director.'

'Reschedule it. And arrange for Juan and Fernando to meet me with the car downstairs straight away.'

Lucia gaped at him, nonplussed. 'And your video call with Peter Reynaud at noon?'

'I'll be back in time for that,' he said, because he had to be. His intended acquisition of Reynaud Industries took priority over everything.

Buttoning his jacket, he turned to go.

Lucia shot up from her chair, her expression vaguely panicked. 'But where are you going?'

'To deal with a problem,' he replied, and strode towards the lifts, leaving his wide-eyed, slack-jawed secretary staring after him.

Barcelona was basking in the heat of a blazing sun beneath a glorious blue sky when Jordan emerged from the hostel just before eleven a.m. She'd risen late and then lingered over breakfast, chatting with a Canadian guy and a young German couple who'd wanted to ask her a bunch of questions about Australia.

Pausing on the pavement outside the hostel, she rummaged in her tote bag for her sunglasses and slid them on. She had a mild headache, and her ears still rang from the overloud music in the club last night, but at least she wasn't suffering with a hangover. She'd had one tequila shot with the girls, then stuck with lime and soda water for the rest of the time.

The dancing had been fun, but the clubbing scene wasn't really her thing. She'd only gone because the two Irish girls with whom she was sharing a room had invited her out, and the prospect of a few hours of deafening music and fun-loving company had appealed more than sitting alone feeling sorry for herself.

'Senyorita Walsh?'

She looked up, startled, when she saw a burly man she didn't know in a suit and dark glasses standing in front of her. 'Yes?'

'Senyor de la Vega wishes to speak with you,' he said, and then gestured towards a vehicle sitting at the kerb. 'Please get in, *senyorita.*'

Shifting her stunned gaze from the man to the SUV, Jordan wondered how she hadn't noticed the vehicle sooner, given that it was bigger and shinier than any other in the street. Black paintwork and dark windows gave it a slightly sinister veneer, and she couldn't see who, if anyone, was sitting inside it. Another man of solid build stood by the rear door, which sat open, waiting for her to climb in.

Her heart beginning to pound, she bounced her gaze back and forth between the two men and the tiny hairs on her arms lifted. They were strangers, asking her to get into a car, supposedly sent by a man she barely knew.

She backed away. 'Actually… I—I have somewhere else to be right now… Maybe Mr de la Vega could call—hey!'

Suddenly the man's meaty hand was wrapped around her arm. Her heart tripped with panic and her brain could scarcely compute what was happening before she was tugged forward and bundled unceremoniously into the back of the SUV. She sucked in her breath, ready to scream, but the sound died in her throat as her backside landed, rather inelegantly, on soft leather and her gaze fell on the man sitting farther along the seat.

'Good morning, Ms Walsh.'

Her pulse spiked. Hastily she righted herself, dismayed to find when she looked down that her wrap-around skirt had got twisted beneath her and was gaping open, exposing the length of one pale thigh all the way up to her crotch. A fierce blush scalded her cheeks.

Lips tightly pursed, she closed the offending split with an indignant tug. 'I'm not sure it is a good morning, Mr de la Vega.'

The car door closed behind her, shutting her in. Making her acutely aware of the confined space and the potency of the man whose presence seemed to fill every inch of the luxurious interior.

Breathing deeply, she willed her heartbeat to slow and tried not to look as overheated and flustered as she felt. How did he do it? How did he look so cool and refined in his immaculate three-piece suit and tie when the day was stiflingly hot and everyone else was melting?

Not that she could entirely pin the blame for her stampeding pulse and all-over body-flush on the rising mercury or the few seconds of fright his men had given her. But she would *not* think about how ridiculously handsome Xavier de la Vega was. Or how he looked not only cool and urbane in his sleek designer suit but also supremely fit and virile.

One dark brow slanted up. 'Late night?'

Striving for an air of dignified calm, she folded her sunglasses away and pushed back some strands of hair that had slipped from her ponytail and fallen across her face. 'Not particularly,' she said, crossing her fingers at the tiny lie.

Technically it hadn't been a late night but rather an extremely early morning when she'd finally collapsed into her narrow bunk bed in the hostel. As for her roomies—Lord knew what time they'd eventually crept in. They'd both still been fast asleep as of ten minutes ago, one of them lying face-down and fully clothed on top of the bedding. If the girl hadn't been softly snoring, Jordan would have felt compelled to check that she was breathing.

She lifted her chin. 'I was referring to the fact that

I hadn't planned on getting manhandled into a car this morning.'

He frowned. 'You were hurt?'

For a second she was tempted to say yes, just to test his reaction, see if he was capable of demonstrating remorse, but she wasn't that good a liar. 'No,' she said, because the man who'd held her had been strong, but not rough, and the only thing truly smarting was her pride. 'But that's beside the point.'

'Which is…?'

She saw a flicker of movement at one corner of his mouth that looked suspiciously like amusement. 'My point,' she said, prising her gaze away from those firm lips, 'is that this is a rather unorthodox way of meeting. You couldn't have called me first?'

'Forgive me,' he said, but his tone and the eloquent shrug of his broad shoulders gave the impression he didn't care one way or the other whether she did or not. 'Given the way you came to my office in person last night, I assumed that you'd prefer face to face.'

What I'd really prefer is to wipe the superior look off your face.

The thought rushed into her head from out of nowhere, and the small surge of churlish pleasure she gained from it was quickly overshadowed by shame. She'd never hit another person in her life—had never been so much as tempted to before now. Perversely, the fact that he'd so effortlessly provoked her into thinking about slapping him only made her feel ten times more annoyed.

She considered explaining that she wouldn't have turned up at his offices as she had if Lucia hadn't blocked her calls and denied her an appointment, but she chose not to go there. She hadn't warmed to the leggy brunette, but she had no desire to get the woman into trouble with her boss.

She sighed. 'Look, I know we didn't exactly get off on the right foot—'

'Which I regret,' he cut in, his voice growing deeper, more solemn.

She blinked. 'You do?'

'Yes,' he said evenly, 'and it is something I would like to redress, if you would allow me to.'

And it struck her then—belatedly. She'd been so blindsided, so caught up in her reaction to him, she'd failed to consider the obvious. 'You believe me,' she said, not a question but a statement—because why else would he be here? 'About Camila.'

'Yes,' he said again. 'I believe your late stepmother was my birth mother.'

Emotion more powerful than she'd expected drew her throat tight. She swallowed. 'I... I'm glad,' she said, wanting to say more, so much more, but holding back. His demeanour was calm, imperturbable, but she read the tension in his clean-shaven jaw, saw the slight guardedness in his silver-grey eyes.

And she understood. It was a big thing to process. Eventually he'd be ready. He'd want to know more about Camila, and then Jordan would have the opportunity to share her memories. To talk about the warm, generous woman who'd been her stepmom and best friend for half her life.

'You must allow me to show you some genuine Catalan hospitality,' he said. 'I have a villa on the coast where my housekeeper is preparing a guest room for you as we speak. It is yours for the duration of your stay in Barcelona.'

Jordan stared at him in stunned astonishment. Last night he'd greeted her with open suspicion and barely veiled hostility, and now he was inviting her to his home?

For a moment she wondered if *she* should be suspicious of *him*.

But why?

He'd candidly expressed his regret and now he'd extended an olive branch. Wouldn't she do the same? If she'd behaved poorly, regretted the way she'd treated someone, wouldn't she make an effort to set things right?

She hesitated. Was there any good reason she shouldn't accept his offer?

You're attracted to him!

Okay. There *was* that small, undeniable fact. But what of it? There wouldn't be a heterosexual woman on the planet who could meet this man and not feel some level of physical attraction. And that was all it was, she assured herself. A hormone-based reaction to a good-looking man at the height of his prime.

Beyond his looks he wasn't her type, and a man who could have his pick of the world's most beautiful, sophisticated women wouldn't be interested in her anyway. Which meant those surges of heat, the pinpricks of awareness she'd experienced last night and again today, were best ignored for a whole host of reasons—not least of which was the preservation of her pride.

She bit the inside of her lip. None of this changed the fact that he was arrogant and presumptuous—as evidenced by having a guest room prepared for her before she'd even accepted his invitation!

But, no matter how impossible it seemed, this man

was Camila's biological son. Did she not owe it to her stepmom to give him another chance?

If she accepted his offer, stayed as a guest in his home, they'd have an opportunity to talk properly—not in his office or the back of a chauffeured car, but somewhere more comfortable and private.

Plus, she still had the letter. *His* letter, by rights. At some point she'd have to relinquish it.

She released her lip and smiled with genuine gratitude. 'Thank you. I'd like that very much.'

The smile she got in return was no more than a brief lift of one side of his mouth, but his grey eyes gleamed with… She wasn't sure what, exactly. Satisfaction?

He gave a crisp nod, then raised his left hand to the window beside his shoulder and rapped the backs of his knuckles twice on the tinted glass.

Seconds later, as if by magic, Jordan's door swung open.

'Juan will help you with your things,' he said. 'I trust it won't take you long to pack?'

She glanced out, saw the long, trouser-clad legs and polished black boots of the man who'd 'escorted' her to the car, then looked back to Xavier. 'We're going *now*?'

His gaze was steady. 'Is that a problem?'

'Er…no,' she said after a slight hesitation. 'I—I guess not…'

She supposed it made sense. The car was already here. And she was travelling light, with a single large backpack, so she wouldn't need more than a few minutes to gather her things.

The big man with the mountainous shoulders—who seemed no less intimidating even now that she knew his name—waited in the reception area while she went to pack. The Irish girls were still out for the count, so she moved about the room quietly and left a farewell note, saying she was checking out due to a change of plans and she wished them well on their travels.

When she emerged, Juan reached for her backpack. 'Let me carry it, Senyorita Walsh.'

Although she was more than capable of carrying her own bag, she gave it up without argument. He was under orders, and she suspected even a burly, tough-looking man like Juan would not wish to invite his boss's displeasure.

'I just need to settle my account,' she told him.

'It is done.'

She frowned. 'But—'

'Please come at once, *senyorita*. Senyor de la Vega does not like to be kept waiting.'

Jordan wasn't happy about it, but she held her tongue. Arguing with the hired muscle was pointless. She would say something to Xavier, though. She couldn't allow him to pay her hostel bill. It didn't matter that she'd pre-paid the accommodation and the outstanding charges had just been for a few incidentals. It was the principle that counted. And while she wasn't one to hold a grudge, neither would she forget in a hurry the stinging assumptions he'd made about her motives. The last thing she wanted to do was give him any reason to cast such aspersions on her again.

But when she got to the car, this time thanking the other man who opened the door, she couldn't say as much to Xavier because he had his phone pressed to his ear and was conversing with someone in Spanish or Catalan.

She hesitated, wondering if he'd prefer privacy, but

he beckoned her in with a perfunctory wave of his hand. Then he continued his conversation as if she wasn't there.

Which was fine, she told herself as she settled back against the cool leather, carefully arranging her skirt to avoid another incident of indecent exposure. It was Friday, the middle of a working day for him. She could raise the issue of the hostel bill later.

Besides, there was something deliciously indulgent about simply sitting there, listening to that deep, molasses-rich voice of his. His tone was brusque and authoritative, suggesting the call was work-related rather than personal, but still she found his voice utterly mesmerising. And she didn't have to feel uncomfortable about eavesdropping. Besides the odd word she could translate, she didn't understand what he was saying.

'*Un moment*,' she heard him say, and translated that in her head: one moment.

Then she heard, 'Belt up,' and it took her a few seconds to realise he'd spoken in English. Another few to register his silence.

Suddenly her senses prickled. She jerked her gaze from the view outside her window to the man beside her and found his grey eyes fastened on her intently.

A jolt went through her midsection. 'I'm sorry—were you speaking to me?'

His eyebrows snapped down. 'Seatbelt,' he said, and when she didn't immediately move he made an impatient sound in his throat, put his phone down between them and reached across her.

Three seconds. That was how long it took for him to pull the belt across her front and secure the latch, yet still her pulse leapt and her breathing fluctuated wildly as she pressed back against the seat. Somehow he avoided touching her—not even a brush of his long fingers against her clothing—but his face came so close she felt the warm stroke of his breath on her collarbone and caught the subtle scents of sandalwood and something citrusy on his skin.

She swallowed—hard—and he must have heard for his gaze settled on her throat, right where she felt the frantic beat of her pulse. His eyes became hooded and for just a second, no more, his gaze dropped, skimming down the front of her white V-necked T-shirt, then up again.

Their eyes locked and something flashed in his, something hot and furious, almost accusing, that she didn't understand.

Then, abruptly, he pulled back, snapping his gaze away from her as he picked up the phone and resumed his conversation.

Dragging her gaze off his hard profile, Jordan let out a shaky breath. Had she done something wrong? Aside from forgetting to put her seatbelt on?

She glanced down and— *Oh…*

Oh, no…

Was that what he'd seen? The clear outline of her hardened nipples thrusting like little beacons of desire against her cotton bra and T-shirt?

Heat suffused her face. Mortified, she folded her arms over her breasts.

For heaven's sake. What was *wrong* with her? With her body? It wasn't as if she'd never met an attractive man before. Her ex, with his square jaw, dark blond hair and deep blue eyes, had always drawn more than his share of female attention and probably still did.

But Josh had always had to touch her—intimately—
to induce this sort of powerful, conspicuous reaction.

If Xavier could have this effect without even touching her, what would happen if he actually put his hands
on her?

She hugged her arms more tightly over her chest.
Spontaneous combustion came to mind.

Which was silly as much as it was unsettling. She
didn't even believe in this sort of thing. Not really. Plain
old physical attraction she understood, but the much
more abstract concept of chemistry…? Not so much.

Whenever she'd heard sex described with words such
as *explosive* and *mind-blowing* and *electric*, she'd always dismissed them as exaggeration or pure fiction.
Sex with Josh had been enjoyable for the most part, but
she didn't remember ever feeling any lightning strikes
of sensation or 'explosions' of pleasure. Orgasms for
her had been a rather hit and miss affair—secondary
to Josh's release—and on the occasions when she had
climaxed it had been satisfying, but hardly a 'mind-
blowing' event. And, because Josh had seemed to know
what he was doing, she'd never imagined there was
much more to sex beyond what she'd experienced with
him.

Anyway, sexual chemistry was supposed to be a
mutual thing, wasn't it? Whatever she'd glimpsed
in Xavier's eyes had looked more like anger than
arousal—or maybe even disgust. Which was morti-
fying on a whole other level. Clearly he was not attracted to redheads with modest curves and pale skin
covered in too many freckles.

That conclusion was enough to douse any lingering
heat—for which she was grateful. Who wanted to feel

attracted to someone who very obviously didn't fancy them back?

No, thanks. She'd learned at the tender age of six how much rejection hurt. Twenty years later she knew better than to make herself vulnerable to that kind of pain again. She'd made a mistake with Josh, but she'd been smart enough to realise it and *she* had been the one to walk away. And although her heart had felt a bit bruised, and she'd shed a few tears, she hadn't ended up bitter and disillusioned.

She *knew* that good men existed in the world because her dad had been a gentle, loving man. She simply had to make wiser choices when it came to relationships and men.

Mr Right was out there somewhere.

And he most certainly wasn't the man sitting beside her.

Some eight hours later Jordan woke from a nap she hadn't planned on having. Memory crept in slowly, reminding her where she was, so when she opened her eyes she wasn't startled by the unfamiliar surroundings.

She sat up on the bed and noted the shallow angle of the sunlight slanting into the room, suggesting the sun had commenced its evening descent. She checked her watch and *was* startled to find she had slept for well over an hour.

She hadn't meant to sleep at all. She'd only intended to lie down for a minute or so, just long enough to determine if the ornate iron-framed canopy bed, with its diaphanous white curtains and the thick mattress layered in soft snowy linens, was as comfortable as it looked.

It was.

And she had never slept in anything so luxurious. Or so enormous.

It must have been the sheer comfort combined with the fresh air and exercise she'd enjoyed that afternoon that had sent her off to sleep.

She scooted off the bed, walked barefoot over sumptuous pale carpet to the French doors that led to a private balcony and stepped out to appreciate the magnificent view.

From here she could see the path she'd taken on her solitary walk after lunch, zigzagging down no less than six beautifully landscaped terraces to a white strip of sandy beach at the foot of the hill.

Directly beneath her lay the longest section of the wide natural stone terrace that wrapped around three sides of the villa, complete with an inviting infinity pool and the shaded alfresco area where she'd eaten the scrumptious lunch Rosa had prepared for her—which, aside from the housekeeper's brief appearances to check everything was okay and to clear away the dishes, had been another solitary affair.

She hadn't been all that surprised when Xavier had returned to work rather than accompanying her to his villa. Everything she'd read about him painted him as focused and driven, so there were probably very few things that would lure him away from his work responsibilities on a weekday afternoon.

This morning, in the car, he'd only ended his call as they'd pulled up outside the Vega Tower. 'My housekeeper, Rosa, will greet you at the villa and get you settled in,' he'd said, his tone impeccably polite, and then he and Juan had got out, leaving just her and the driver.

Jordan would have tried to chat with the man if not

for the dark glass partition between them. Instead she'd focused on the scenery as they'd exited the city, her interest sharpening when, after about thirty minutes, they'd started to climb, weaving up and up through large, sloping groves of olive and citrus trees until finally they'd levelled out at a location that offered glorious views across the glittering blue of the Balearic Sea.

Rosa had appeared on the stone steps at the villa's entrance before they'd even drawn to a stop. The fifty-something housekeeper had a neat salt-and-pepper bob and a broad, welcoming smile, and she hadn't seemed at all fazed by receiving a house guest at short notice.

She'd shown Jordan her room and given her a tour of the main living areas, all of which were light and spacious and luxurious beyond anything she'd ever seen. The grounds were beautiful, too. Outside on one of the upper terraces Rosa had introduced her husband, Alfonso, who worked as the chief groundsman, and their grown-up nephew, Delmar, who was helping his uncle with some landscaping.

The whole place was gorgeous. And tranquil. A home only a billionaire could afford.

Too bad he probably spent more time at work than here, enjoying his amazing home.

Turning away from the stunning view, she went inside and took a shower in the massive en suite bathroom, and afterwards pulled on a pair of navy dress jeans and a short-sleeved white blouse. She hadn't thought to ask Rosa about the dress code for dinner, and she'd never dined with a billionaire in his home before, so 'smart casual' seemed the safest option.

After tying her hair into a loose knot at her nape, she checked the time and decided to make an appearance ten minutes earlier than Rosa had recommended. If her host was a stickler for punctuality she'd rather be early than even a minute late.

The villa was so big she took two wrong turns on her way to the formal dining room before she finally located it. Pausing in the hallway, she touched a hand to her hair, took a deep breath and then walked into the room. Rosa was there and Jordan smiled at her, then shifted her gaze to the long dining table—and the single place-setting at one end.

Before she'd fully processed the implication of that single setting, Rosa said quickly, '*Ho sento, molt.* Senyor de la Vega sends his apologies. He must work late.'

Her heart sank. After all the nervous anticipation, discovering she would be dining alone—again—was a huge let-down.

Seeing Rosa's anxious expression, however, she made an effort to resurrect her smile and said lightly, 'That's okay. Perhaps I'll catch him later, when he gets home.'

Rosa wrung her hands together. 'I am afraid he is not coming home tonight.'

She looked at the housekeeper in surprise. 'He's staying at work all night?' she said, yet even as she spoke she knew it wasn't inconceivable that someone like him would work through the night and into the weekend. He was a workaholic, and workaholics had only one priority.

'He has an apartment above his office,' Rosa said. 'He stays there often. Senyor de la Vega works very hard,' she added, and Jordan couldn't tell from Rosa's tone whether she admired or disapproved of her employer's work ethic.

She regarded the table again. Despite the fine china and the sparkling crystal, the gleaming cutlery and the beautiful vase of crimson calla lilies, the solitary setting looked rather forlorn at the head of the enormous table.

'Rosa, would it be all right if I ate outside on the terrace?'

Out there she'd at least have the birds and the crickets for company. And she could gaze out to sea and watch the sun as it sank below the horizon.

The housekeeper smiled. '*Sí*. Of course.'

An hour later Jordan sat on the terrace in the gathering dusk with a full tummy and a glass of white wine, watching the sky turn to lush shades of orange and purple. She could hear laughter and snatches of conversation coming from somewhere nearby. The feminine voice she recognised as Rosa's; the male voices no doubt belonged to Alfonso and Delmar.

She pictured the trio, enjoying their own alfresco meal, and the sounds of their banter sharpened the sense of isolation that had crept over her in the last hour.

She took a gulp of wine. Was this what Xavier had intended all along? To isolate her?

Suddenly his offer of hospitality didn't seem quite so munificent.

But why? Was he somehow testing her? Had he left her up here to see what she would do? What did he *think* she would do? Pocket the silverware? Slip some crystal into her bag? Snatch a priceless painting off the wall and hightail it off the estate before she was found out?

More laughter danced through the still air and she swallowed another mouthful of wine.

She knew this hollow feeling in her chest. It was loneliness. And she refused to let it suck her down into a place of misery. She didn't do self-pity. Self-pity was a waste of time. She'd learnt that as a child in the wake of her mother's departure, when she'd realised that crying under the duvet wasn't going to bring her mother back. She had dried her eyes, got out of bed and focused on the parent she still had. She'd made herself indispensable to her father.

Because if Daddy needed her then he wouldn't go away. Wouldn't leave her like Mummy had.

Jordan shook off the childhood memories. It was history, and dwelling on the past was just another form of self-pity. The best medicine for the blues was to do something, and with that thought in mind she got to her feet, picked up her wine glass and went in search of the laughter.

CHAPTER THREE

IT WAS CLOSE to one-thirty p.m. on Saturday when Xav arrived home—a couple of hours earlier than he'd anticipated. He grabbed his briefcase, dismissed his driver for the remainder of the weekend and strode into the villa.

He should be dead on his feet. He was operating on little more than two hours' sleep and a gallon of caffeine. But he wasn't exhausted. He was wired. It was how he always felt in the midst of a major business deal. Focused. Determined. *Ruthless*.

It put him in the perfect frame of mind to deal with a certain redhead—a problem he would have tackled sooner, had Peter Reynaud's bloodsucking lawyers not waited until six p.m. last night to return their marked-up version of the one-hundred-and-fifty-page contract. Either they were tearing every damn clause and sub-clause apart to eke out their billable hours, or Reynaud himself was hindering the process.

Furious, Xav had made his commercial and legal teams pull an all-nighter—which meant he'd had no choice but to stay as well. He never demanded anything of his people he wasn't willing to demand of himself.

At least he'd been able to focus one hundred percent on work, secure in the knowledge that his other 'problem' was safely contained for now. Offering up his villa had been a stroke of genius, and she'd played into his hands just as he'd thought she would. Few women could resist the lure of luxury—especially when the luxury was free.

All he needed now was her signature on the paper-work in his briefcase. Once executed, the confidentiality agreement would prohibit her from disclosing any in-formation about the biological relationship between her late stepmother and himself to any third party. In return she would receive a handsome one-off payment—a sum Xav considered a small price to pay for peace of mind. The last thing he wanted was some tabloid journalist digging up the answers to questions he had decided a long time ago he didn't want to ask.

As for that one minor glitch yesterday—that fleet-ing moment of hot, naked lust that had struck him un-awares in the car, when he'd leaned across her to belt her in and her light, feminine scent had curled around him... He'd glanced down, away from those entrancing hazel eyes and soft, full lips—away from *temptation*—only to be transfixed instead by pert breasts and hard, pointed nipples poking shamelessly against the fabric of her T-shirt, just *begging* for his attention.

Lust and fury had collided. Fury at her for tempting him; fury at himself for *being* tempted.

Subsequently, his having to stay overnight in the city had been a blessing in disguise. For a few hours he'd been able to cast her out of his head, shrugging off the incident as nothing more than the base reaction of a neglected libido.

Pausing now in the villa's double-height entry hall,

he pulled off his sunglasses and waited, listening for Rosa's approach.

Nothing.

Which was unusual.

His housekeeper of ten years had an uncanny radar for people arriving at the villa—particularly her employer.

He moved deeper into the house and then stopped, canting his head.

He could hear music.

More specifically, the jaunty strains of the *gaita*— the Galician bagpipes that Rosa's husband, Alfonso, had a talent for playing. He heard voices, too. And laughter.

Frowning, he set his briefcase and sunglasses down, followed the sounds through the house and ended up standing outside the kitchen, looking across Rosa's meticulously tended herb and vegetable gardens to the staff cottage where she and her husband lived.

Xav recognised the music now—an old folk song— and it was indeed Alfonso on the *gaita*. He sat in the shade of a massive orange tree at a wooden table littered with the detritus of a group meal, his wiry chest puffing in and out as he breathed life into the old instrument. Rosa sat beside him, smiling and clapping, but it wasn't the housekeeper who held Xav's attention—it was the couple on their feet.

Alfonso's twenty-something nephew, Delmar, who helped his uncle with the odd stint of landscaping on the estate, was performing the steps of a traditional folk dance, while opposite him Jordan Walsh attempted to mirror his moves.

Xav couldn't tear his gaze off her—and it was no wonder, given the clingy tank top and denim cut-offs she wore. The latter left bare the long, slender thighs he'd caught a tantalising glimpse of in the car yesterday, before she'd closed her skirt in that prim display of modesty.

She laughed, the sound surprisingly throaty and appealing, and tossed her head, drawing his gaze to that magnificent mane of copper-red hair with its streaks of glinting gold. She wore it down today, and it flowed over her bare shoulders, thick and wavy, the ends softly curling against the pale upper slopes of her breasts.

Heat punched into his groin, swift and brutal in its intensity, and he gritted his teeth against the unwanted surge. *Dios.* His libido had lain dormant for too many months to count and it was springing to life *now*? In response to *this* woman?

She messed up her steps and laughed that husky laugh again, and then she stumbled and Delmar's big hands wrapped around her waist to stop her falling.

Xav wasn't fully aware that he'd moved—that he'd stalked between the neat borders of the vegetable patches and crossed to the cottage—until suddenly he was standing in the yard, the music had stopped and four startled faces were staring at him.

'*Senyor!*' His housekeeper leapt to her feet with remarkable agility for a woman of her age. 'We were not expecting you so soon.'

'Clearly.' His response came out sharper than he'd intended, but the way they were all staring at him made him feel like an interloper—an outsider in his own home. He didn't like it.

'Can I fix you some lunch?' Rosa offered.

'*Sí.* A sandwich will do. I'll take it in my study.' He turned to Jordan and noted with a stab of satisfaction that Delmar had removed his hands from her body and stepped away. 'Ms Walsh,' he said evenly, and she looked at him with what he thought might be a touch of defiance in her hazel eyes. 'A word in private, please—if you can spare a moment from your dancing lesson.'

Giving her no chance to reply, he turned on his heel and strode back to the villa, detouring to where he'd left his briefcase and collecting it before heading to his study. Assuming she was trailing somewhere not far behind, he didn't slow his pace or glance over his shoulder until he reached the doorway, where he finally paused and looked back—only to see she was nowhere in sight.

His mouth flattened.

Infernal woman.

He dumped his briefcase on the desk, returned to the hallway and cast an impatient look down its vast, empty length.

Finally, just as he was beginning to consider the possibility that she'd decided to defy him, she emerged around a corner at the far end of the hallway and, spotting him waiting, hurried towards him on those long, shapely legs. She stopped in front of him, panting a little, each breath moving her firm, high breasts up and down.

He gritted his teeth. *Don't look.*

'Did you get lost?' he said dryly.

'Of course I got lost.'

Her snapped response made him draw back a fraction. 'I was being sarcastic.'

She gave him a droll look. 'Were you? I would never have guessed.'

She jammed her hands on her hips and huffed out a breath, blowing an errant strand of hair out of her face.

'If you actually care to know, I *did* get lost. You stormed off so quickly I couldn't catch up and I took a wrong turn at the kitchen. I didn't know which way you'd gone and this place is…is ridiculously huge.'

Xav took in her flushed cheeks, the cross look on her face and her generally flustered demeanour. A sudden flash of amusement drew the sting out of his temper.

He cocked an eyebrow. 'You think my home is ridiculous?'

Her eyes widened, her expressive features morphing into a look of dismay. 'Of course not!' she blurted, her blush turning a deeper shade of pink. 'I only meant… I meant I wasn't…'

She bit her lip, which had the dual effect of halting her stammered response and drawing his attention to the lushness of her mouth—which in turn fired a pulse of heat into his groin and hampered his ability to concentrate when she took a deep breath and spoke again.

'You have a very beautiful home,' she said, enunciating her words slowly this time, as if selecting each one with care. 'An amazing home, actually. It's just that my sense of direction is hopeless and…well, the villa *is* rather…'

She fluttered her hand in the air, searching, he assumed, for a suitably inoffensive word.

'Big?' he supplied helpfully.

She cleared her throat, her cheeks glowing like hot embers now. 'Yes.'

A crueller man would have let her squirm for a bit longer, but he wasn't quite that merciless. Plus, he had no idea where this urge to tease and provoke had sprung from—or, more dangerously, where it might lead—so he was better off shutting it down. The fact that she'd already had him lurching from arousal to anger to amusement and back to arousal again in the space of mere minutes, when usually he was so adept at governing his emotions, was disturbing enough.

He motioned her into the room, followed her in and then closed the door and crossed to his desk.

'I hope you're not angry with Rosa and Alfonso and Delmar,' she said.

He turned and looked at her. She stood in the middle of the room, her colour still high, her arms folded tightly over her breasts.

'Do I have reason to be?'

She frowned at him. 'I don't know. Why are you asking me? You're the one who marched in looking as if you wanted to throttle someone.'

He *had* wanted to throttle someone. Delmar. An urge for which he could offer no reasonable explanation. All he knew was that he hadn't liked seeing the younger man's hands on her. The familiarity between them. What else besides dancing had they got up to over the last twenty-four hours?

Had she encouraged him?

Pain arced through his jaw and he realised his teeth were clenched. Relaxing his expression, he sat against the edge of his desk and crossed his ankles. Good manners would normally dictate that he offer the lady a chair, but he wasn't feeling especially chivalrous just then.

And he rather liked having her standing there in the centre of his antique Persian rug where he could see her.

All of her.

He could tell it made her uncomfortable and he enjoyed that—perhaps a little too much.

Maybe he *was* that cruel.

He folded his arms loosely over his chest. 'I'm not accustomed to finding my house guests fraternising with the staff.'

Her chin came up. 'Perhaps your staff wouldn't have had to entertain your house guest if their employer hadn't been an absentee host. If anything, you should be thanking them. Rosa has been wonderful—and Alfonso. They've very generously shown me some of that Catalan hospitality you promised.'

'And Delmar?' he couldn't resist asking.

Just how generous had his *hospitality been?*

Her brow scrunched. 'Of course. Delmar, too. They've all been exceptionally kind. I hope you know how lucky you are to have them,' she added, her tone implying that she considered him entirely unworthy of his employees' services.

Well, well... It seemed his little nurse from Down Under was a zealous defender of others.

Xav stilled.

His little nurse...?

His jaw tightened again.

Jordan Walsh was not *his* anything.

He unfolded his arms and pushed away from the desk. Time to end this conversation. He'd already derived too much enjoyment from their exchange. There was a reason he wanted her here and it wasn't for fun.

The fact that this brief exchange had not only aroused his libido but stirred a gut-deep feeling within him that Jordan Walsh was a woman of candour, who lacked the guile to harbour any sort of hidden, materialistic agenda, however, was an irony not lost on him.

Which left him...*where*, exactly? Saddled with a

house guest he couldn't turn out—not without having to wage a battle against his conscience. He didn't deny he could be ruthless when a situation demanded it, but he never compromised his principles. Never took any action he couldn't justify unreservedly.

Righteous was what his younger brother had called him many times over the years—usually when Xav was taking him to task over some louche, ill-disciplined behaviour.

But Ramon would never understand. How could he? His veins ran with the blood of their parents. The blood of generations of Spanish aristocracy and even royalty. He'd never had to endure those sideways looks. The snide, disrespectful comments.

Admittedly when they were teenagers Ramon *had* beaten the living daylights out of their cousin Diego, after overhearing him call Xav a mongrel, but Ramon had been just as furious at Xav for refusing to engage.

And *that* was what Ramon failed to understand. That Xav couldn't afford to lower himself to his tormentors' level. He had to be better. In every way possible. Maintaining a solid moral compass, ensuring his reputation was unimpeachable—that was what gave him the ability to rise above his detractors and prove to himself as much as to anyone else that he was the better man.

Yesterday he'd used the pretext of regret to coax Jordan Walsh into accepting his offer of hospitality. It had stretched his moral boundaries to do so, but he'd acted without compunction and would do it again. She'd been an unknown quantity, which had made his actions both justifiable and necessary.

And it wasn't as if she could claim mistreatment or hardship. He had done her a favour, surely, plucking her out of that hostel and installing her in the luxury of his home. The only reason she had her pretty nose out of joint now was because she felt neglected.

'It is unfortunate that I could not be here last night,' he said, the words as close to an apology as he was willing to offer. 'I am sure you can appreciate I have a company to run and there are times when work must take priority. You are right,' he added. 'I am fortunate to have good employees. I knew Rosa would make you comfortable in my absence.'

Deciding that now was not the ideal time to present her with the nondisclosure agreement, he walked to the door and opened it.

'I look forward to seeing you at dinner this evening, Ms Walsh. In the meantime, I have more work to do. So if you'll excuse me…?'

She gave him a long, silent look, and for a few seconds he had the unwelcome sensation of being laid bare. As if those extraordinary hazel eyes could cut to the core of him and see all the flaws and defects that he'd secretly feared existed ever since he was a boy.

Then she blinked, and the strange sensation was gone, and in the next breath so was she, breezing past him and out of the room without a word.

As he closed the door a bitter taste formed on his tongue and his throat caught on a dry swallow.

It had been a long time—ten years, to be exact— since a woman had looked at him in a way that made him feel inadequate. The feeling, he discovered, was no less unpalatable now than it had been then.

That evening Jordan devoted more time and effort to her appearance than she had the night before, showering early so she had plenty of time to wash and blow-dry her hair, then putting on the only dressy outfit she'd brought: gold silk palazzo pants and a black satin halter-neck top. She even applied some make-up, blending her freckles with light foundation, darkening her lashes with mascara and adding a touch of cherry gloss to her mouth.

She didn't do any of it to impress Mr High-and-Mighty. It was all for her: to boost her confidence, give her an extra layer of protection—like armour—so she wouldn't feel as bare and vulnerable as she had today, when he'd made her stand in his office like a naughty schoolgirl hauled in front of the headmaster for a telling-off.

He'd been *so* arrogant. So unbearable. And so infuriatingly, breathtakingly handsome in his pressed trousers and crisp shirt while everyone else had looked hot and ragged, herself included.

His only concession to it being the weekend had been the rolled-up shirtsleeves, the absent tie and the five o'clock shadow—and even *that* had somehow looked immaculate.

Xavier de la Vega might have been born to the daughter of a humble farmer, but he was in every way that mattered besides blood an aristocrat.

And a jackass. At least he had been today—having a go at her for *fraternising* with his staff. She refused to believe he was such a snob that he considered the people who worked for him too lowly to socialise with. It didn't fit at all with how Rosa and Alfonso spoke of him. The few times they'd mentioned him in conversation their comments had always reflected an unwavering loyalty and a deep respect for their employer.

No. Something else must have triggered his animus. She just didn't understand what.

Sighing, she slipped her bare feet into a pair of strappy black heels.

Maybe it was just her. Maybe they were destined to rub each other the wrong way.

Which made her heart clench on a pang of regret. She hadn't imagined her relationship with Camila's son would be so...antagonistic.

Or so *incendiary*.

Because, even knowing her pride was at serious risk, she couldn't pretend those little detonations of heat that occurred beneath her skin when she was near him weren't disturbingly real.

It was all very well trying to ignore her body's response to him, but today, as she'd stood in his office and found herself on the receiving end of a very frank, very masculine appraisal, the inevitable flash of heat and awareness had been so overpowering she'd feared he would see some evidence of it.

Even more disturbing had been the trick her imagination had played on her. Or maybe it had been a trick of the light reflecting in those cool grey eyes that had, for a brief moment, made them look blisteringly hot and molten.

Then, to unbalance her completely, there'd been moments when his hostility and surliness had abated and a kind of dry, reluctant amusement had surfaced.

It was all terribly confusing.

And overwhelming.

No wonder her stomach was jumping with nerves as she made her way downstairs.

At least she didn't make any wrong turns on her way

to the formal dining room tonight, having finally got the layout of the villa successfully memorised. She paused in the hallway, as she had last night, and touched a nervous hand to her hair, then walked into the room—and pulled up short.

It was empty.

She looked at the long, polished dining table. There were *no* place settings tonight.

'I thought you might like to dine outdoors.'

The deep voice came from behind her and she spun round, a hand splayed over her startled heart.

'Apologies,' Xavier said, one side of his mouth tilting up. 'I didn't mean to frighten you.'

She smiled and shook her head, even though her heart continued to race. In a silk shirt the same shade of steel-grey as his eyes, and dark trousers that hugged narrow hips and long, powerful legs, he looked devastatingly attractive. *Again.* His dark hair was swept off his forehead and he'd shaved since she'd last seen him, leaving his tanned jaw hard and smooth.

'It's fine,' she said, feeling a little breathless. 'And, yes, outdoors sounds great.'

He guided her through a set of French doors at the far end of the dining room and onto the terrace, where a table was beautifully set for two. The summer sun had begun its descent towards the horizon and the warmth of the evening was tempered by a light breeze off the ocean.

He held out a chair for her. 'Rosa mentioned that you'd chosen to eat out here last night, so I thought you might like to do the same this evening.'

She sat down, her awareness of him behind her manifesting itself as a hot, tingling sensation feathering down her spine. As he moved away to take his own seat she caught the same scents of sandalwood and citrus that she'd picked up on yesterday, in the back of the car.

'Thank you,' she murmured, feeling surprised and a little bit wary that he was being so...*nice*. She cleared her throat. 'Did you get all your work done this afternoon?' she asked politely.

'My work is never done.'

She discerned a wry note in his voice, but no hint of resentment or self-pity. He simply sounded matter-of-fact.

He lifted a bottle from a silver ice bucket on the table. 'Wine?'

'Yes, please.' She waited until he'd filled their glasses and returned the bottle before speaking again. 'Is that why you work six days a week?'

'Seven sometimes.'

He grabbed his napkin, snapped it loose and placed it over his lap, performing the simple task with the same precision she imagined he applied to every task he undertook.

He looked at her and paused, one dark eyebrow angling up. 'I take it from your expression you disapprove?'

Hot colour bloomed in her cheeks. Was she so easy to read? 'I don't disapprove of hard work,' she said, sorting out her own napkin and then picking up her knife and fork.

Their starters were already on the table: dainty salads of dark green arugula, with melon, pistachios, crumbled goat's cheese and thin, delicate strips of a cured meat. She speared a cube of melon.

'But...?'

She glanced up, straight into his piercing grey eyes, and felt her pulse kick. 'Focusing on work to the exclusion of all else isn't very healthy,' she ventured. 'Life should ideally be a balance of things—work, leisure, relationships, family...' She paused. 'You must want a family of your own one day?'

She winced inwardly as soon as the question was out. What on earth had made her ask that? It was too personal. She braced herself, waiting for him to suggest she mind her own business.

He surprised her. '*Sí*. And when I have a wife and children it will be my responsibility to provide for them.'

His words immediately conjured an image in her head of a brood of beautiful dark-haired little children, romping through the hallways of this enormous house.

Camila's grandchildren.

'Of course,' she said, putting down her fork and reaching for her wine, conscious of a sharp, painful pang in her chest. 'But once you've got kids you won't want to work all the time, will you?'

'I'm CEO of a multinational corporation with a multibillion-dollar turnover,' he said, in that very matter-of-fact tone again. 'I will never have the luxury of a mere forty-hour working week. Which is why I will select a wife who'll be content to focus on my needs and our children's.'

The quintessential corporate wife. *Of course.* Jordan could just picture her, too. She'd be elegant, poised, well-dressed and well-bred—because an impeccable pedigree would be a must—and, of course, stunningly beautiful. Oh, and she'd be the consummate hostess, handing off the children to the nanny while she hosted lavish dinner parties for her husband's friends and associates, naturally at ease in these sumptuous surroundings and never once getting lost in the sprawling maze of marble-tiled corridors and rooms.

Jordan swallowed a large sip of wine. The very thought of the future Mrs Xavier de la Vega made her feel horribly, utterly inferior.

'You might fall in love with a career woman,' she couldn't resist suggesting.

'If my future wife has a career she will need to juggle her priorities and ensure our children come first.' He picked up his own wine and savoured a mouthful before continuing. 'And when I marry it will be for compatibility, not love,' he said, sounding about as passionate as if he were discussing the purchase of a fridge.

The hopeless romantic in Jordan balked. Not marry for love? Love was the *only* thing she would marry for. She knew what a loving, committed relationship looked like. It was what her dad and Camila had had, and she wanted the same for herself. And children, of course. What could be more rewarding, more satisfying, than surrounding yourself with people to love and nurture? People who *needed* you?

As for expecting his future wife to prioritise her children over her career—Jordan would be hard pressed to argue the flipside of that coin. Maybe because she remembered what it was like to be the child of a workaholic parent. Knew the deep, long-lasting hurt and eroded self-worth that resulted from being abandoned by a mother who'd been more interested in climbing the corporate ladder than raising and loving her child.

No…the idea of a woman devoting herself to her children, making them a priority, didn't sound terrible at all.

'You disapprove of this too?'

She put her wine glass down. 'How can you say you won't marry for love?'

He shrugged a broad shoulder. 'Marriage is a union between two parties—not unlike a business partnership—and the success of any partnership relies on common goals and values, not whimsical emotion.'

So cold and clinical. And so wrong! Love wasn't whimsical. Love and true emotional commitment were the only things strong enough to weather the inevitable ups and downs of life.

His attitude to the contrary cast a chill over her skin.

She turned her attention to her salad, as did he. Which was good. *Safe.* Subjects they disagreed upon were best left alone.

Except Jordan just couldn't help herself. 'So…if you're always working…and you're not interested in taking the time to look for a love match…how exactly will you find a wife? Pay someone to do it for you?' she said, half jokingly—and then she saw the flare of dull red across his cheekbones.

Uh-oh.

He reached for his wine, took a sip, then set the glass back down, each movement unhurried. Controlled. He would have looked utterly imperturbable if not for the tiny muscle flickering in his jaw.

'Do you find that concept strange, Ms Walsh?' he said at last. 'The idea of hiring a proven professional who can handpick a shortlist of candidates whose needs, goals and desires perfectly align with your own?'

She flushed. 'No, I don't think it's strange. I know there's plenty of matchmaking services out there, and that plenty of people avail themselves of such a service.

I'm just not convinced it really works. Or that it's the best way to find your life partner.'

'Is there a better way?' he challenged smoothly. 'Or do you prefer to leave your relationships to chance?'

She felt the flush spread down her neck. Just because that approach hadn't worked out so great for her so far, it didn't mean it never would. 'I prefer to think the right guy is out there somewhere, and that when the time is right I'll meet him.'

'Ah.' His lips gave a cynical twist. 'Destiny?'

'Something like that,' she said, sounding a bit prickly and hating it that she did. 'But I'd prefer *that* to choosing someone based on a clinical checklist of goals and attributes.' She sipped her wine, the crispness of the Sauvignon mingling with the sudden bitterness on her tongue. 'And if you have children?' she asked. 'If you don't love their mother will you love them?'

Xavier went very still all of a sudden. 'What sort of question is that?'

A perfectly valid one, she thought defensively, given that he'd declared his idea of a successful marriage was one devoid of love! His children would be her stepmom's grandchildren, and a part of Camila would live on in them. Was it unreasonable for her to want to know if those children would grow up happy and loved?

Just then Rosa appeared, interrupting the awkward moment to deliver a main course of chargrilled peppers and slow-roasted lamb. She cleared their first course plates and set out new ones, giving no indication of whether she sensed the tension between her boss and his guest.

'*Gràcies.*' Jordan managed a smile for the housekeeper. 'That salad was delicious, Rosa.'

She beamed. 'You are welcome, *senyorita.*'

Rosa left and for long minutes they each concentrated on their meal. Twice Jordan opened her mouth to speak, desperate to break the oppressive silence, but both times she lost her nerve at the last second and shovelled a piece of lamb into her mouth instead. Luckily the meat was exceptional—unlike her floundering conversational skills. But how did one backpedal from loveless marriages and children to polite, inconsequential small talk?

'Why did you become a nurse?'

Xavier's deep voice carved through the heavy silence. Jordan lifted her gaze, startled by the fact he'd spoken as much as by the question itself.

'How do you know I'm a nurse?'

'Rosa mentioned it.'

'Oh.'

So he'd had a conversation about her with his housekeeper? Or maybe Rosa had just mentioned it in passing. Rosa had told her that her and Alfonso's only daughter was a nurse, married and working in Berlin, so Jordan had naturally mentioned that she too was a qualified nurse.

'It's the only job I ever wanted to do. Right from when I was a small child,' she said, smiling because she couldn't *not* smile when she talked about her chosen profession.

Taking care of people wasn't just what she did—it was who she was. Who she had been from the day her mother had walked out and her bewildered father had needed his daughter to step up.

'I can't remember a time I *didn't* want to be a nurse.'

He picked up the wine bottle and refreshed their glasses. 'And why trauma?'

She sat back, lifted a shoulder. 'It's fast-paced, high-pressure… You're helping people—that's the most important thing, of course—but it's also…*exciting*.'

Just thinking about it made her blood pump a bit faster. The only time she didn't love her job were the days when a patient died. Those days were a brutal reminder of the fragility and brevity of life. A reminder that you had to make the most of every moment and appreciate the people you loved, because sometimes they were gone too soon.

Xavier's voice broke across her thoughts. She blinked and swallowed down the little lump that had lodged in her throat. 'Sorry?'

'Do you work in a major hospital?'

'I did for several years. In Sydney, in one of the country's best accident and emergency departments.'

She'd loved that job. Had been so proud to work in that particular trauma centre. She'd beaten over a hundred other applicants for the position.

She hesitated before adding, 'But I resigned a few months ago and returned to Melbourne.'

'So you have a job there?'

She hesitated again. They were venturing into more sensitive territory now, but this was ultimately what she wanted, wasn't it? A chance to talk about Camila…? And yet last night she'd lain awake in that beautiful canopied bed, sleep eluding her, and in a moment of gut-wrenching doubt had wondered if bringing Camila's letter to Xavier had been an act not of kindness but of cruelty.

Because how must he feel? To have learnt of his birth mother's identity and at the same time learnt that she'd passed away and he'd never have an opportunity to meet her?

And yet what had been the alternative? To throw the letter away? Pretend it didn't exist? Jordan couldn't have done that.

She took a deep breath and said quietly, 'No. I moved home so I could nurse Camila through her final months. She had leukaemia,' she explained, a sharp ache hitting the back of her throat.

She glanced down, away from his probing gaze. She hated revealing her grief. She preferred people to see her as strong and resilient—because she *was*.

'You nursed her full-time? Alone?' His voice was quiet now, too.

She looked up and tried to gauge his expression, but couldn't tell what emotion, if any, lurked behind his silvery gaze. 'Yes.'

'That's quite a sacrifice.'

She shook her head. 'I didn't see it like that. Camila was family. There was never any question in my mind that I would nurse her when the time came.' She was silent a moment. 'Camila was so strong and brave. She didn't want me to give up my job, and was upset for a few days when I did. But I don't regret it. The time we had together at the end was special. I'd do it again.'

'A leave of absence wasn't possible?' he queried.

'No. I didn't know how long I'd need. I couldn't expect the hospital to hold my job open indefinitely. And I thought I might need a break afterwards, anyway. Time to sort out a few practical things.'

Like the family house, which she'd spent a few weeks clearing and tidying but hadn't yet decided whether to sell or keep.

'Before Camila got sick we used to talk about doing a trip to Spain, but we never did. After she died, I decided to come on my own.'

She stopped short of telling him that she'd brought Camila with her. That her stepmom's ashes were upstairs in a small urn and she planned to scatter them into the vast blue of the Mediterranean Sea as soon as she found the perfect spot. Or that—before she had met him—she'd entertained the possibility of inviting him to join her in that act.

She sipped her wine, put the glass down and pushed it slightly away. Too much alcohol would dull her brain. And there was something niggling in her head, floating at the periphery of her thoughts. Something not quite right...

Suddenly icy fingers of realisation gripped her insides. She looked at Xavier. 'How did you know I'm a trauma nurse?'

The widening of his eyes was so slight she almost missed it. Then his expression became inscrutable. He put his cutlery down. Slowly.

A sinking sensation slid through Jordan's stomach. 'I told Rosa I'm a nurse—I didn't mention I specialised in trauma,' she added, the words scraping her throat like coarse sandpaper.

His gaze locked with hers and the look in his grey eyes was unflinching. Unyielding. *Unapologetic.*

'You had me investigated,' she choked out, and he didn't deny it. 'Why?' she demanded—but then she raised her palm in a 'stop' gesture. 'You know what? Scratch that. I already know the answer.'

'Calm down,' he said smoothly. *Condescendingly.* Which only fanned the flames of her ire.

'Don't tell me to calm down. From the second we met you've questioned my motives. My integrity. Do you honestly expect me *not* to feel offended?' She straightened her shoulders and channelled her indignation into a lofty glare. 'You don't even know me.'

'Precisely, Ms Walsh.' A hint of steel underpinned his voice. 'I do not know you. And I will not apologise for taking precautions to safeguard the interests of myself and my family.'

She let out a humourless huff of a laugh. 'You're unbelievable.' She slapped her napkin onto the table, pushed back her chair and stood.

'Sit down,' he commanded. 'We're not finished.'

She balled her hands into fists. She could feel her anger building now, pushing at the walls of her chest, searing her veins with heat. It strengthened her backbone. Diminished the likelihood of her embarrassing herself with stupid tears.

'We *are* finished, Mr de la Vega. Or at least *I* am.'

She glanced down at her unfinished meal, at the food Rosa had so beautifully prepared and served. With a pang of regret, she turned away and strode into the house.

CHAPTER FOUR

Xav managed to restrain himself for a full minute before he flung down his napkin with a muttered oath and went after her.

He scowled at his own idiocy. He rarely made mistakes, but he'd blundered right into that one.

Where the hell had his head been at?

He climbed the stairs, trying to recall which guest suite he'd told Rosa to put her in, and then remembered. The suite at the south end of the villa—as far from his own sleeping quarters as possible.

Finding the door shut, he rapped his knuckles twice on the wood and waited.

Nothing.

'Ms Walsh,' he called out.

He could hear faint sounds of movement from inside the room, but the door remained closed.

Damn it.

'Jordan!'

Pinching the bridge of his nose, he raised his fist to knock again.

The door jerked open.

Luminous golden-green eyes glittered angrily at him. 'I'd be grateful if you or Rosa could please call me a taxi.'

'No.'

Her eyes narrowed and then she whirled away and strode towards the bed, where a haphazard pile of toiletries and clothes lay next to her open rucksack. 'Fine,' she muttered. 'I'll ask Rosa myself.'

She was still wearing the outfit she'd worn to dinner, and the swish of gold silk around her long legs and the snug fit of the black top against her high, full breasts stirred the same response of masculine appreciation in him now as when he'd first clapped eyes on her downstairs.

Ruthlessly he quashed his lust and moved into the room. Jordan turned, holding up an envelope, and his gut clenched.

'I'm not convinced you're ready for this,' she said. 'But it's not mine to keep. I hope you'll treat it with the respect it deserves.'

She placed it on the nightstand, then picked up a wallet, pulled out some euros and tossed them onto the end of the bed. 'For the hostel bill.'

She started shoving items of clothing into her bag, her movements jerky and stiff. The only part of her that didn't look rigid was the long silken fall of her magnificent copper hair.

'Stop,' he said.

But his tightly voiced command fell on deaf ears.

She dropped a pair of canvas shoes on the floor, pulled off her high-heeled sandals and jammed them into her rucksack.

He stepped closer. 'Jordan.'

She paused and looked up, and for a second he saw everything in those stunning hazel eyes. Everything she was feeling and struggling to hold in: anger, disappointment, hurt.

It made his gut clench again. *Hard.*

'I think it's best if I go,' she said, her voice quiet, and then she resumed her packing.

Frustration surged and he reached out a hand and grasped her wrist. She froze instantly, her entire body stilling, and he wondered if she'd felt the same jolt of electricity as he.

Gently he turned her to face him, the pulse in the soft underside of her wrist beating erratically against his thumb. 'Stay.'

Her chin rose in challenge. 'Why? So you can keep an eye on me?' Her tone was a mix of hurt and reproach. 'That's the reason you invited me here, isn't it?'

She tugged her wrist but he held firm, not yet ready to let her go. Enjoying the contact too much.

'I stand by what I said,' he told her, but in a gentler tone than he had used at the table. He had been harsh, more so than was necessary perhaps, but he hadn't enjoyed finding himself in the altogether discomfiting position of having to defend his actions. 'I will not apologise for being cautious.'

She made an indignant sound in her throat and turned her face away.

Lifting his free hand, Xav brought her chin back round with his thumb and forefinger. 'But I have upset you,' he continued, 'and for that I am sorry.'

Her eyes widened, although whether in surprise at the apology or at the dominating touch of his hand, he didn't know.

Whatever the cause, it didn't erase the look of stubborn pride from her face. 'You only want me to stay because you don't trust me.'

He dropped his hand from her chin, before the urge to drag the pad of his thumb across her bottom lip— to see if it felt as lush and soft as it looked—grew too strong to resist.

'That's not true.'

It wasn't a lie.

She was bold and unexpected. From the moment she'd turned up at his offices the other night, spouting the outrageous claim that she was his stepsister, through to today, when he'd come home and discovered her laughing and dancing with his staff, he'd felt as if his carefully controlled world was shifting beneath him.

And tonight… Somehow she'd turned even the act of sharing a meal into an unpredictable affair. How the hell they'd ended up talking about marriage and children and *love*, of all things—that singularly destructive emotion he had vowed to avoid at all costs—he had no idea.

Irritation had made him want to reassert control, turn the focus back onto her.

Earlier in the day, when Rosa had delivered his sandwich, he'd casually elicited her opinion of their guest, and in the midst of her effusive praise of the younger woman she *had* mentioned that Jordan was a nurse. At dinner he'd used that, and then deliberately asked questions that would trip her up if her answers didn't correspond with what he already knew from the investigator's report.

Instead he had tripped himself up, and he hadn't even realised his mistake. He'd been too spellbound.

Too captivated by the enthusiasm and passion she exuded when she talked about her work.

And then she'd spoken of her stepmother—*his* birth mother—and her compassion and the sacrifice she'd made to nurse the woman through her final weeks of life had made him feel unexpectedly tight-throated and humbled.

The gut feeling he'd had this afternoon had strengthened into certainty. This woman was no threat.

She tugged her arm again and he realised he was still holding her. Reluctantly he let her go, and as she stepped back, her arms wrapping around her middle, it occurred to him he could let her go altogether. He could let her pack her bag, put her in a taxi as she had asked him to do and send her on her way. He could write all of this off as an unfortunate disruption and get on with his life.

Simple. Practical. Convenient.

So why could he feel his chest tightening and his body tensing in rejection of the idea?

Why did he feel as if he wanted to soothe the look of hurt and vulnerability from her face while at the same time a part of his mind was entertaining dark, carnal thoughts that involved dragging her onto the bed, stripping her naked and doing things with his hands and mouth that would make her forget about leaving and have her begging him instead to let her stay?

Dios.

Never before had a woman provoked such a tumult of conflicting urges in him. Not even Natasha, the ice-blonde American heiress who ten years ago had left him deeply embittered, determined never again to make himself vulnerable to that kind of humiliation and pain.

Clenching his jaw, he thrust her cold, heartless, duplicitous image out of his head and focused instead on the hot, stubborn, fiery woman in front of him.

'Then why?' she challenged. 'Why do you want me to stay?'

He pinched the bridge of his nose between his thumb and forefinger, then dropped his hand. 'Because right now you're the only connection I have to the woman who gave birth to me,' he said.

The admission made him feel a little raw inside, even though it was only part of the truth as to why he wanted her to stay—the only part that made enough sense to try to explain. And even that was difficult, because he'd never expected to feel curious about his birth mother. Up until forty-eight hours ago she'd never been anything more than a faceless, nameless woman—and then Jordan had walked into his office and shown him a photo. Told him a name. Camila Walsh, nee Sanchez. The woman who'd given birth to him at eighteen and thirty-five years later died of leukaemia. A woman whose stepdaughter had loved her enough to sacrifice her job so she could nurse her through her final days.

He didn't know how he was supposed to feel about all that. He certainly had no hope of articulating it. So he didn't even try.

'I don't think you want to sever that connection just yet any more than I do,' he hazarded instead, and watched a look of telltale uncertainty shift across her face.

Trapping her voluptuous bottom lip between her teeth, she glanced towards her half-packed rucksack, then back to him. 'If I stay,' she said, a slight emphasis on the *if*, 'would you consider coming somewhere with me tomorrow?'

Had he not been distracted by her mouth again, Xav

would have registered the distant clang of alarm bells as he responded. 'Where?'

There was a pause. 'I want to visit the village where Camila grew up.'

He jerked his gaze up to connect with hers, the lush perfection of her lips momentarily forgotten.

'It's north of here,' she rushed on, before he could even properly assimilate what she was asking. 'Up the coast and then inland towards the mountains. About a two-hour drive, according to Delmar.'

His gut suddenly tensed. 'He knows—?'

'Of course not,' she interrupted, frowning at him. 'That's your personal business. I would never share that information with anyone else. I just mentioned at lunch that I wanted to visit my stepmom's village and asked for advice on travel times.'

Advice she could have sought from him instead of Delmar.

If you'd been here.

He clenched his back teeth together.

'Camila didn't have any living relatives left in Spain,' she went on. 'So you wouldn't have to worry about… you know… Running into someone you're related to…' She trailed off and was silent for a moment. 'Look, I'll understand if you're not interested. But I'm going anyway. I was planning to hire a car, but Delmar has offered to drive me—'

'No.' The word shot from his mouth like a bullet from a gun he hadn't intended to fire.

She blinked. 'Okay…' Her voice was tinged with disappointment. 'I understand…'

He doubted she did, because *he* sure as hell didn't. Admitting curiosity about his birth mother was one thing. Traipsing up the country to visit her birthplace was quite another. But the alternative—Jordan spending the day with Delmar...

'No,' he repeated. 'You misunderstand. I mean Delmar will not be driving you. I will.'

Her eyes went wide. 'Really?'

'Sí,' he said, and the smile that broke out on her face then was so radiant his heartbeat lost its rhythm for a moment.

She brought her clasped hands beneath her chin and rose on her toes, and for a second he thought she was going to do something unexpected like lean in and hug him.

Hastily he stepped back, the mere thought of her soft body pressed against his making his blood heat and that huge bed beckon enticingly.

A fine layer of sweat broke out on his skin. 'I'll have Rosa bring a tray with your dessert. Given that we'll be out tomorrow, I'll need to do some work this evening. I will see you in the morning. I'll ask Rosa to serve breakfast at eight,' he said, and pivoted on his heel.

'Xavier.'

Hearing her speak his forename in that soft, husky voice of hers pulled him up short, in spite of his eagerness to retreat.

Reluctantly he turned and she came towards him, that damned envelope in her hand.

'You should take this,' she said.

He hesitated and weighed his options. Reject the letter and risk shattering that soft, hopeful look on her face, or take it and keep the peace?

He took it.

In his study, he dropped the envelope on his desk, went to the sideboard to pour a drink and came back to his desk to sit down. He swallowed a mouthful of brandy and shifted his gaze from the envelope to the manila folder containing the confidentiality agreement he'd left out in readiness on the corner of his desk.

A clear vision filled his head of Jordan ripping the document into pieces and hurling them in his face.

He finished his brandy in one large gulp, then grabbed the folder and shoved it into a drawer, slid the envelope in after it and slammed the drawer closed.

One day, he told himself as he opened his laptop and made a start on his emails.

One day he would read the letter his birth mother had written to him.

But not tonight.

The scenery along the stretch of coastline known as the Costa Brava was breathtaking. Jordan had grown up in a small coastal township south of Melbourne, so she was used to ocean and beaches, but the glittering shores of the Mediterranean were in a different class altogether. Each time the sleek convertible powered around another bend, and a new stunning vista opened up before them, she couldn't suppress a little gasp of awe.

Another one caught in her throat now, and Xavier glanced over from the driver's seat.

'Spectacular, *si*?'

He was spectacular. As riveting as the scenery in faded jeans and a loose-fitting white shirt with an open collar and rolled-up sleeves. Stubble shaded his jaw and she liked this edgier look on him. He wore dark sunglasses, and his thick black hair was deliciously ruffled thanks to the car's open top.

Every time she looked at him her breath went a little choppy, but it was the moments when he smiled—when his mouth loosened and those deep, attractive grooves appeared in his lean cheeks—that her breath was snatched away completely.

'Stunning,' she agreed, and with an effort peeled her gaze off him and looked out of her side of the car, feeling slightly giddy as she peered down the steep pine-covered cliffs that plunged into the sparkling blue water below.

She'd woken this morning with a tiny glow of optimism in her chest that she was determined to cling to as tightly as she could.

Last night when she'd stormed away from the table she'd been so mad at Xavier, and so determined to leave. She'd felt hurt and exposed, and she'd wanted to stay angry at him, but he'd made it so difficult—or at least that was what she'd told herself as she'd climbed into that gloriously comfortable bed and felt a stab of guilty relief that she wasn't climbing into a narrow bunk in a hostel room shared with strangers.

But the truth was she had been a hopeless push-over, losing the battle from the moment he touched her, when the anger pulsing in her veins had morphed into a very different sort of heat.

And then he'd tipped up her chin and said he was sorry. That the word *sorry* even existed in his vocabulary should have shocked her, but she'd barely noticed the apology. She'd been too distracted. Too busy watching him look at her mouth and too stunned by the knowledge of what she was witnessing in his eyes.

Heat.

Desire.

Hot, prickling awareness had washed over her, settling in the pit of her belly and leaving traces of heat long after he'd left the room.

This morning, as she'd made her way down to breakfast, which Rosa had laid out buffet-style on the terrace, her pulse had still pounded unevenly and she'd wondered what she should do with that knowledge.

Ignore it?

Pretend she hadn't noticed?

Try to forget that she'd lain in that big bed last night and dreamt of shocking, inappropriate things that were guaranteed to make her blush furiously when she next saw Xavier?

Easier said than done.

And, yes, heat *had* swarmed her face—along with other, less visible parts of her body—when she'd walked onto the terrace and found him already there, sitting at the table with his long legs stretched out in front of him and his dark hair and bronzed olive skin gleaming in the sun.

He'd held an espresso cup in one hand and a palm tablet in the other. As she'd approached he'd looked up and said, *'Buenos días.'* Then he'd enquired how she'd slept and poured her a cup of eye-wateringly strong coffee.

It had all been perfectly polite and pleasant, and that was all. There'd been no heated looks. No lingering gazes. Nothing to suggest that he hadn't walked out of her room last night and either forgotten the moment instantly or dismissed it as being of no significance.

And it was a relief. Really, it was. She hadn't come to Europe looking for a holiday fling, even if her friend Ellie *had* said that it was precisely the kind of liberating, no-strings fun she needed after enduring the toughest few months of her life.

No. She was taking a month to travel, with a list of things to do and see, and then she was going back to Australia to build a new life, since most of her old one was, sadly, now gone.

Anyway… If she were looking for a holiday romance she wouldn't be setting her sights on a man who was as arrogant as he was sexy—and who happened to be her stepmom's son!

The car swept around another bend and she shifted to look at the satnav on the dash.

'Another hour,' Xavier said. 'If you want a drink or a restroom there's a town a few miles ahead.'

'No. I'm fine, thanks. Unless you need a break…?'

'I'm good.'

His eyes were focused on the road, so she let her gaze linger on him for a bit. Just because their relationship would only ever be platonic, at best, it didn't mean she couldn't appreciate that he was a magnificent-looking man.

He looked totally at ease in the driver's seat of the Aston Martin—as competent and self-assured at the wheel of this sleek, powerful machine as he was at the helm of his family's multibillion-dollar business.

Jordan wasn't a car enthusiast by any stretch, but she had to admit that this morning, when Xavier had driven the shiny silver sports car out of its garage into the sunshine, and then lowered the roof, the prospect of riding in the luxurious convertible with the top down had sparked a tiny thrill of excitement.

'What, Jordan?'

His deep voice startled her from her thoughts and

at the same time sent a shiver racing across her skin. Before last night she'd wished he would call her by her first name; today she wished he wouldn't. Something about the way his mouth framed the word, combined with the sound of his rich, accented baritone stroking over the syllables, was altogether too...*sensuous*.

'What?' she returned innocently.

'You were looking at me.'

Her face heated. 'You're looking at the road. How can you possibly know what I'm looking at?'

The muscle at the corner of his mouth flickered, hinting at amusement, and her pulse leapt in her veins. They were both making an effort to get along today, and even though the light mood felt a bit forced it was ten times better than the way things had been between them yesterday.

A part of her was still astonished that he'd agreed to come with her. Last night her heart had clenched at hearing him finally admit that knowing who his birth mother had been meant something to him, but a niggle of doubt had made her wonder if he'd just been telling her what he thought she wanted to hear. Asking him to do this trip with her had been a challenge—a test of sorts—to see if his curiosity about Camila was genuine.

'What were you thinking?' he asked now.

'How do you know I was thinking anything?' she countered, feeling a tug at the corners of her own mouth.

Every now and again over the last two hours they'd slipped into a comfortable banter which she was finding dangerously addictive. Xavier in a bad mood was formidable; in a good mood he was downright lethal.

He glanced at her. 'There's always something going on in a woman's mind.'

She pushed her sunglasses up the bridge of her nose. 'That's because we're highly intelligent.' And then, re-alising she'd just cornered herself with that statement, she added, 'If you must know, I was thinking you look remarkably relaxed today.'

'"Remarkably"?'

She shrugged. 'You know what I mean.'

'No,' he said smoothly. 'Enlighten me.'

She shot him a sidelong glance. 'Well…you're not exactly the most laid-back person in the world.'

A sharp, narrow bend loomed ahead and he slowed and shifted gears. 'Is that your way of sugar-coating what you really want to say?'

They rounded the bend and he accelerated out of it onto a long, straight stretch of road.

'That's my way of being polite.'

'And the less polite version?'

She clamped her lips together.

'Jordan?' He pressed her with a look.

She held out for a few seconds more, then capitu-lated with a sigh. 'Fine. You're a chronic workaholic. Which means you're *not* relaxed most of the time. You're uptight, probably have a skewed set of priori-ties, and you would benefit from taking a chill pill once in a while.'

'A "chill pill"?'

'Metaphorically,' she clarified. 'I don't condone recreational drugs.'

She saw the muscle in his cheek flicker again, and it suddenly annoyed her that he seemed to find her amus-ing when she wasn't trying to be.

'Should I brace myself for another lecture on work/life balance?'

Feeling a touch defensive now, she lifted her chin and pointed out, 'You *did* ask. And, if I recall correctly, you're the CEO of a global corporation with a multibillion-dollar turnover who doesn't have the luxury of a mere forty-hour working week,' she said, quoting his spiel from last night back to him verbatim. 'I suspect any lectures on work/life balance would be completely wasted on you.'

His lips quirked again, and for one pulse-hitching moment she thought he was going to break into one of those lethal smiles that were guaranteed to leave her breathless.

Then he cast her another look and his mouth suddenly flattened. The car decelerated so rapidly her stomach pitched.

She braced her hand on the door as he braked to a stop on the hard shoulder of the road. 'What's wrong?'

He pulled his sunglasses off, his gaze narrowing on her face. 'You said you were wearing sunscreen.' His voice was a low, accusatory growl.

She frowned. 'I am.'

He jabbed a button on the console and the car's roof emerged from its housing.

She made a sound of dismay as it closed over their heads, blocking out the glorious sunshine. 'Why did you do that?'

'Your nose is sunburnt.'

'Oh.' *Was that all?* She shrugged a shoulder. 'That will teach me for buying the cheap stuff—' she touched her forefinger to the end of her nose '—and for having a big nose,' she joked.

His mouth thinned. 'Your nose is perfect.' He pushed his sunglasses back on and set the car in motion again.

'And you have beautiful skin,' he said gruffly. 'You should protect it.'

A burst of warmth flared in Jordan's chest at the unexpected compliments, despite how tersely they'd been delivered. She willed herself not to blush, but felt the colour rise in her cheeks regardless.

'Look who's lecturing now,' she said lightly, attempting to cover her silly overreaction to a couple of abrupt remarks. 'It's kind of nice, though,' she added, settling back against the seat and casting him a sideways glance, 'you being all…protective. When I was little I used to dream of having a big brother who'd look out for me.'

His jaw tightened. 'Jordan…' he warned in a low, gravelly rasp that should have deterred her but instead sent a hot quiver through her belly.

Catching her tongue between her teeth, she bit down—literally—on the reckless impulse to see how far she could push him in this mood. Chances were his growl was worse than his bite. But she wasn't quite brave enough to find out.

An hour later Xav leaned against the side of his car, ankles crossed, arms folded over his chest, his mind stuck on a single word like a turntable needle stuck on scratched vinyl.

Protective.

He clenched his jaw. If what Jordan provoked in him was protectiveness, it sure as hell wasn't of the brotherly variety.

Dios.

The sibling reference had been nothing more than a taunt, surely? She couldn't possibly be oblivious to the fact that the subtle, provocative two-way baiting and constant simmering tension between them was sexual chemistry.

When she had strolled onto the terrace this morning, wearing a stretchy yellow-and-white-striped dress that was little more than a thigh-length T-shirt, the hot surge of reaction in his gut had been anything but *brotherly*.

With her flame-coloured hair swept into a high, bouncy ponytail, her long legs smooth and bare and her feet encased in cute white tennis shoes, she'd looked like a burst of summer sunshine. A sexy, irresistible package of ebullience and warmth.

He'd known in that moment this trip was a bad idea, but he wasn't a man who reneged on his promises. And, while he'd avoided analysing too deeply his feelings about what they were doing today, he wasn't insensitive to the fact that visiting this village where he now stood, in the green forested foothills of the Catalan mountains in the middle of nowhere, meant something to Jordan.

Truth be told, he'd enjoyed their journey up the coast. When was the last time he'd put the top down on his sports car and hit the open road? For that matter, when was the last time he had driven instead of *being* driven? He employed a driver because travelling in a chauffeured vehicle allowed him to work while on the road, but he hadn't realised how much he'd missed getting behind the wheel.

And when had he last consciously appreciated the natural beauty of the Costa Brava, or even his own private slice of the coastline, other than via the window of his jet when he flew in and out of the country on business?

Throw a beautiful woman into the mix—even one who pushed his buttons at every turn—and the result had been a blood-pumping exhilaration that was different from the adrenalin rush he derived from the day-to-day cut and thrust of the business world.

But when they had turned inland his pleasure had begun to evaporate, dwindling with each kilometre that had brought them closer to this dull, isolated backwater.

As he'd parked at the foot of an ancient cobblestoned street, a sobering, unwelcome revelation had struck.

This was the place his biological roots could be traced back to. This sleepy, remote village that looked as if it had got permanently stuck in some bygone era.

He suppressed a shudder.

Even as a boy, given to fleeting bouts of curiosity about his biological parents, he'd not once imagined his beginnings to be so…*inauspicious*. As a teenager he'd stopped wondering altogether—any shreds of curiosity ruthlessly crushed, his focus one hundred percent on proving himself worthy of the name he carried to this day with a fierce sense of loyalty and pride.

A feeling of claustrophobia pressed down like a suffocating weight on his chest, and he wanted to climb into his car and floor the accelerator until the village was nothing more than a distant, inconsequential speck in his rear-view mirror.

Except he couldn't. Because Jordan wasn't with him and he didn't know where the hell she'd gone.

He pushed away from the vehicle. He shouldn't have let her wander off alone. By her own admission her sense of direction was non-existent. But when they'd arrived he'd checked his phone and found two missed calls from his brother and a voicemail mentioning Peter Reynaud.

He'd stayed in the car to call Ramon and Jordan had

stepped out to give him privacy, stating she was going to stretch her legs.

He'd not seen her since.

He stared up the street. His conversation with Ramon hadn't lightened his mood. His brother had got wind of a competitor sniffing around Reynaud's assets. It renewed Xav's suspicions that Reynaud was intentionally stalling their deal.

Voices caught his attention and he glanced up the street to see a middle-aged couple in hiking gear emerging from a small general store. They disappeared down a lane and then the street was empty again.

Blowing out a frustrated breath, he pushed away from the car and started up the street. He'd taken no more than two steps, however, when Jordan bounded out of the store onto the cobblestones and turned in his direction. He stopped and she hurried towards him, her features animated.

'Xavier!'

The impact of her smile combined with the breathless, eager way she said his name made a pulse throb in his groin.

She halted in front of him. 'You won't believe this.'

He almost snorted. If he'd learned anything about this woman over the last couple of days it was to expect the unexpected. Someone should tattoo a warning across her forehead: *Beware: unpredictable.*

He looked into her upturned face. 'What?'

'The couple who own the store knew Camila,' she announced, her eyes, with those extraordinary striations of amber and green, sparkling up at him. 'Can you believe that? They were childhood friends until Camila went to Australia and they lost touch. They're lovely…'

She sank her teeth into her bottom lip and Xav braced himself for whatever was coming.

'They've invited us to lunch.'

A different sort of tension that had nothing to do with desire gripped his insides.

'Please say yes,' she said in a rush, before he could get out a word. 'They won't know that you're related to Camila. I simply told them I'm with a friend.' She stepped closer, latching those big, beautiful eyes onto his. 'Please, Xavier,' she entreated. 'It'd be rude to refuse. And it would mean so much to me.'

Dios. Why did he find it so damned difficult to say no to this woman?

He glanced over his shoulder at the car. For a second he very seriously considered picking her up and throwing her in, locking the doors and driving the hell out of there.

He looked back to Jordan.

Her hands were clasped under her chin now and she looked impossibly cute. Infuriatingly irresistible.

He dragged his palm over his jaw. Expelled a heavy breath. *Damn it.*

'Fine,' he said. 'One hour. No more. And Jordan...?' He waited for her to stop bouncing on her feet and pay attention. 'They do *not* learn about my relationship to Camila. Understood?'

She gave a vigorous nod. And then, without warning, she stood on tiptoes and pressed a kiss to his cheek. 'Thank you,' she said, her voice low and husky, a touch breathless again.

Xav answered with a grunt and then quickly stepped back, his jaw locked.

'Xavier?'

Somehow he managed to keep his eyes off the lips

he now knew were every bit as lush and petal-soft as they looked. *'Sí?'*

'You're scowling.'

He wasn't scowling. He was *concentrating*. Attempting through sheer will to prevent the sudden heat that had lanced his belly from infiltrating other, more visibly reactive parts of his anatomy.

With effort he unclenched his teeth. Ironed out his features. 'Better?'

She tilted her head to the side. 'A bit. Just…smile,' she suggested. 'Try to look friendly.'

She turned and started back up the street, her ponytail swinging like a bright copper pendulum between her shoulder blades, drawing his gaze inexorably downwards to the jaunty swing of her rounded hips and tight buttocks in the short, clingy dress.

His jaw locked again.

Madre de Dios.

Give him five minutes alone with her, he thought darkly, and he'd show her *friendly*.

CHAPTER FIVE

TWO HOURS LATER Jordan sat in the shade of a pergola in Maria and Benito Gonzalez's quaint cottage garden, looking through the pile of photos that Maria had brought to the table with a tray of coffee and sweet treats to finish their meal.

The men had finished their coffee and disappeared fifteen minutes earlier. Benito had asked if he could look at the Aston Martin, having noticed the car through the shop window when they'd first driven into the village.

Xavier had gone one better and offered to take him for a short spin.

Jordan's insides had melted a tiny bit. She'd almost wanted to hug him. For his kindness to the older man. For letting her do this. For keeping the scowl off his face and remembering to smile every now and again.

'You all look so young,' she said, studying an old wedding photo. 'And you and Camila both look so beautiful, Maria.'

Sitting beside her at the table, Maria smiled. 'Mila was beautiful *and* clever. She altered my mother's wedding dress for me and made her own bridesmaid dress.'

Jordan nodded. 'She made my high school graduation gown from a picture I took out of a magazine.'

The memory made her smile. She'd loved that gown. It was the prettiest thing she'd ever worn up until then. Her dad had got all choked up and said she was beautiful, and then she'd cried too, and so had Camila, and they'd all laughed at themselves for being so soppy.

'She made another for my nursing graduation ball.'

Maria reached over suddenly and squeezed Jordan's hand. '*Ho sento molt.* I am so sorry for your loss, *filla el meu.* And so very sorry that I will not see my friend again.'

Jordan's throat drew tight. '*Gràcies*, Maria. I know that one of Camila's greatest regrets was not having visited her homeland again.'

Maria shook her head. 'No one expected her to come back. I am sad we lost touch, but I was happy for Mila when she left and made a new life for herself. She was never quite the same…after she gave up her child.'

Jordan gave a little start of surprise. Maria had talked about Camila over lunch, sharing light-hearted anecdotes from their childhood, but she'd made no reference to her friend's teenage pregnancy—until now.

Seeing the older woman's gentle expectant expression, Jordan said slowly, 'You knew that I knew?'

'*Sí…*'

Maria reached into her cardigan pocket and withdrew a photo she'd obviously kept back from the rest. She held it out and Jordan took it, and her heart started to thump against her ribs.

The young couple in the snapshot were sitting on a sandy beach. They both wore swimming costumes, had wet hair and wide smiles, and their arms were wrapped around each other.

'Oh, my goodness…' Jordan's throat constricted. 'Camila looks so happy…so…' *In love.* 'And he…'

She trailed off. The handsome, dark-haired young man who was staring with obvious affection at the girl sitting on his lap looked just like— *Oh, God.* She bit her lip.

'He looks like your friend, *si*?'

The resemblance was striking. It might almost have *been* Xavier in the photo.

Jordan couldn't disguise her stricken expression. 'Oh, Maria…' she breathed. 'Please don't say anything to him.'

Maria gave her hand another firm squeeze, offering reassurance. Understanding. 'I am an old woman who is very good at keeping secrets—and minding her own business,' she added.

Jordan looked at the photo again. Camila had said so little about Xavier's father, and Jordan had sensed the subject stirred great sadness in her stepmom so she hadn't pressed.

'Do you remember his name?'

'*Sí.* Tomás.'

Jordan's own dad's name had been Tom. It was a funny little coincidence that meant nothing, but it made her smile. 'Can you tell me what you know about him?'

Maria nodded. 'Of course…'

Ten minutes later the men returned, Benito wearing a smile on his weathered face that stretched from ear to ear.

Maria offered more coffee, but after a quick glance at Xavier Jordan politely declined. They'd been there for two and a half hours already—an hour and a half longer than he'd wanted to stay.

She helped Maria take the cups and plates back to the kitchen. When they were alone, Maria pressed the photo of Camila with Xavier's biological father into Jordan's hand.

Jordan's eyes widened. 'Oh, no… Maria, I couldn't.'

'*Sí*. Please,' the older woman insisted. 'I want you to have it. You have given me a gift today—to hear about Mila's life in Australia and know that she found happiness.' She smiled, even as her eyes grew bright with moisture. 'I think she was lucky to have such a wonderful daughter—and I think she would have been proud to see what a fine man her son grew into, *sí*?'

Her own eyes stinging, Jordan hugged her. '*Gràcies*, Maria.'

Minutes later she and Xavier were back in the car and the Gonzalezes had reopened their store.

She fastened her seat belt and her chest felt incredibly tight, as if there was so much emotion expanding inside her she would either have to express some of it or burst.

She put her hand on Xavier's arm before he could start the car, then pulled her hand away as soon as she had his attention, the brief contact with warm skin and crisp masculine hairs leaving her fingertips tingling.

'Thank you,' she said, her voice a little husky. 'That really meant a lot to me. I know we stayed longer than you wanted to—'

'It's fine,' he interrupted, turning his attention away from her to start the car.

'I also realise the situation must have felt a little… weird for you—'

'Jordan.' He cut her off again as he revved the engine. 'I said it's fine.'

She sat back, trying not to feel stung as he navigated them out of the narrow streets of the village and onto the long road that would take them back to the coast through a thick swathe of dark green pine forest.

But it was hard to smother her disappointment completely.

Deep down she'd hoped he too might feel as if the experience had been special, in spite of any understandable discomfort. The chance to sit down with people who'd known his birth mother during her early life, to hear stories that would build a picture of her in his mind... Surely it had made him feel something? Something other than *fine*?

They drove in silence, but Jordan's mind was anything but quiet. Her thoughts spun, veering between her conversation with Maria, the photo in her bag and the fact that Xavier's mood was much more brooding than it had been before lunch.

Finally the silence got to be too much. 'Have you ever wondered about your biological father?'

He sent her a look she couldn't read, and then took so long to respond she thought he wasn't going to answer her at all.

'Not since I was a boy.'

Conscious of the sudden nervous patter of her pulse, she ventured, 'If you had the opportunity to find out who he was, would you?'

'No.'

There hadn't been even a split-second of hesitation.

'Really? Why not?'

Another long pause. Then, 'You mean why would I not want to find a man who got a teenage girl pregnant and failed to take responsibility for his actions?' He adjusted his grip on the steering wheel. 'I would think the answer to that is obvious.'

'Maybe he was just a teenager himself,' she suggested.

'Doesn't matter. If a man is old enough to sleep with a woman, he's old enough to take responsibility for the consequences.'

Jordan thought about what Maria had told her. It *was* possible that Xavier's birth father had deserted Camila. It was also possible he'd never known she was pregnant and that his family had conspired to keep the young lovers apart.

'But what if—?'

'Enough, Jordan.' He spoke tersely. 'Leave it alone. This is not your business.'

The rebuke nettled. As did the implication that she was meddling in affairs that didn't concern her. 'Camila was my stepmother,' she said quietly.

'And my birth mother.' He gritted out the admission, as though he found the truth of it distasteful. 'Who was also foolish and irresponsible.'

Jordan gasped. 'That's not fair! You can't judge and condemn people when you don't have all the facts.'

'The facts don't matter.'

His white-knuckled grip on the steering wheel and the hard jut of his jaw told her he was angry now. But so was she.

'Of course they matter. How else will you understand what happened?'

'Understanding what happened won't change the outcome, or the present. The past is irrelevant.'

She looked at him, aghast. 'How can you say that? It's your own history—'

'Exactly,' he bit out. '*History*. Done and dusted. I have no interest in the past.'

Stunned into silence, she studied the severe lines of his profile for a moment, running her gaze from the black slash of his eyebrow to the proud ridge of his nose and down over the lean terrain of cheekbone and jaw—the same hard, exquisitely sculptured jaw she'd impulsively kissed on the street and then wished she hadn't when a blast of heat and longing had sizzled right through to her core.

She swallowed. She didn't want to kiss him now. She wanted to grab those big shoulders of his and shake the arrogance out of him.

She turned her head away, looked out of her window and managed to hold her tongue for the next forty minutes. Only when Xavier's mobile phone rang for a third time in quick succession did the urge to speak get the better of her.

'Maybe you should stop and take that,' she said, continuing to look out of her window. 'No doubt it's a work call.'

She heard him draw a sharp breath.

'*Sí*. We will need to stop.'

She expected him to pull over straight away, on the side of the road, but he drove on for ten minutes towards the coast, to a small, sunny seaside town where a beautiful church and pretty whitewashed buildings huddled around a sandy bay.

As soon as he'd parked up she said, 'I'll stretch my legs,' and stepped out of the car with a sense of *déjà vu*.

She'd done the same thing back in Camila's village, giving him privacy to make a phone call. Heaven forbid the CEO of the Vega Corporation should take a *whole* Sunday off!

'Don't go far,' he called from the driver's seat, and she slammed the door, saving herself from having to respond to his bossy instruction.

She jammed her sunglasses on and looked around. Whether by chance or design, he'd chosen a spot that gave her a choice of shops and cafés in one direction and a beach in the other.

The beach beckoned, and the instant she took off her shoes and sank her toes into the silky-soft sand her spirits lifted. It was a gorgeous spot, and not overcrowded, with sunbathers and swimmers enjoying themselves without having to compete for their own piece of sea or sand.

She walked a short distance and was tempted to sit down and linger, but the sun was fierce and she didn't have her sunhat. She'd be better off sitting in the shade of a café awning.

She retraced her steps and then bent down to brush off her feet and slip her sneakers back on. She had just finished tying her laces when a football hurtled up the beach towards her, a tall, shirtless young man in hot pursuit. Automatically she stuck her foot out to stop the ball and its pursuer skidded to a halt in front of her.

'*Gràcies.*'

He stooped to retrieve the ball, and as he straightened his gaze travelled up her body, taking her in with unabashed interest from her ankles to her face. He grinned at her and she couldn't help but grin back. He had the ripped physique of a man but she guessed he was in his late teens, and he was hardly threatening.

'*No hay problema,*' she said, borrowing a phrase she'd heard Rosa use.

Her young admirer cocked his head, long dark hair flopping in his eyes. 'You are English?'

'Australian.'

'Ah. Home of koalas and kangaroos, *si*?'

She laughed. 'Yes.'

His grin broadened. 'And beautiful women.'

She laughed again, shaking her head at his cockiness.

He glanced over his shoulder to where his friends—a group of fit-looking young men and bikini-clad girls—stood waiting for him to bring back the ball. 'You would like to come and play, *bonic*?'

Amused, she opened her mouth to decline, but just then a shadow fell across the sand and her nape prickled with awareness.

'Jordan.'

She stilled at the sound of Xavier's deep voice behind her. How had she known it was him before he'd even spoken?

He came and stood close beside her and the prickling awareness migrated to other parts of her body.

'Is everything all right?'

She glanced at him, registered the dark scowl on his face and felt annoyed with him all over again for dampening her day with his bad attitude.

'Perfectly,' she said breezily.

'Then let's go.'

The command—and his obvious expectation that she'd obey—only stirred her anger. A reckless urge gripped her to push back and get under his skin somehow.

She looked at the younger man and shrugged. 'My brother,' she said, on a heavy sigh. 'He can be a little—' she rolled her eyes '—*overprotective.*'

He glanced from her to Xavier, looking confused,

no doubt due to the lack of physical resemblance. He took in Xavier's powerful form, the aggressive stance, then backed away, firing a rueful shrug at Jordan. 'Another time, *preciosa*.'

Jordan waved her fingers at him and then, her bit of mischief complete, strode past Xavier and back along the footpath to the car, ignoring him as much as it was possible to ignore the presence of a thundercloud at one's back.

She reached for the door handle, but her fingers had barely brushed the metal before her wrist was seized and she was spun around unceremoniously and backed against the car.

She gave a startled cry, then an outraged gasp as Xavier whipped off her sunglasses and tossed them onto the roof.

'Hey!' she protested, even as she instinctively knew the welfare of her sunglasses was the least of her worries just then.

He discarded his own, then palmed the back of her skull while his other hand released her wrist and claimed her hip in a hold that was blatantly possessive and intimate.

She stared at him. 'Xavier?' Her voice emerged as a breathless whisper. 'Wh-what are you doing?'

'Making a point,' he rasped.

And then his mouth came down on hers and Jordan felt as if she'd slammed into a wall of electricity, shock and heat consuming her so completely she could do nothing more than tremble and burn under the savagery of his kiss.

And it *was* savage. Like no other kiss she'd ever experienced before. A kiss of anger and dominance and control. It should have horrified her, incensed her, but there was something sinfully sensual, darkly exhilarating, about the way his firm lips moved with such brutal purpose over hers.

She made a sound she told herself was protest but feared was actually acquiescence. Heat stung her body in places he wasn't even touching. And where he did touch… She felt branded. *Claimed.* By his hands. His mouth. Even the scrape of his thick stubble on her skin seemed like a deliberate attempt to mark and punish.

Never in her life had she been kissed with such utter, breathtaking mastery.

Her mouth yielded under the relentless pressure of his and he went deeper, angling his head and prising her lips apart, stroking his tongue boldly against hers so the combined tastes of coffee and almonds and virile male burst in her mouth like an intoxicant, dangerous and shocking and yet oh-so-delicious.

A deep, responsive shiver rippled through her muscles, and she thought she felt a similar shudder go through him. But then, abruptly, he tore his mouth off hers, throwing her into a state of dazed confusion.

'I am not your brother.'

It took a moment for her shellshocked brain to comprehend what he'd said. Still holding her trapped between the car and his body, he shifted his weight until suddenly the hard, unmistakable ridge of his full male arousal pressed against her belly.

'Do not test me,' he said, his voice a low rumble of warning, 'and expect me to behave as if I am.'

Clamping her upper arms, he moved her sideways, then released her to open her door.

Heart pounding, hands trembling, she retrieved her

sunglasses from the roof and pushed them onto her face. She should say something, she thought weakly, balling her hands at her sides. Something assertive, something to express the anger and indignation she should be feeling—*was* feeling, she corrected herself. But in that moment, with her mind still reeling and her body feeling strangely deprived now that he'd moved away, all she could focus on was getting herself into the car before her knees gave out.

The drive back to the villa took an age. A wall of silence had descended, thick and unscaleable, and Jordan could think of nothing to say to breach it.

Nothing that wouldn't betray how deeply shaken she felt.

Xavier had *kissed* her.

More, he'd revealed his arousal in a manner so blunt and brazen she should have been scandalised. But instead she'd been turned on. And she couldn't stop thinking about it. Couldn't stop remembering how his mouth had felt on hers. Couldn't forget his taste. Couldn't stop replaying that kiss, in all its brutal, breath-stealing glory, over and over in her head.

But the most disturbing thing of all was the hot blaze of yearning in her belly.

Xavier had kissed her.

And she wanted him to do it again.

He shouldn't have done it.

Xav pinched the bridge of his nose and cursed himself for the hundredth time since they'd got back to the villa. He shouldn't have kissed Jordan the way he had, with anger and arrogance and a dark compulsion to punish.

And yet he'd be lying if he said he hadn't enjoyed every damned second of plundering those soft, hon-eyed lips.

She'd enjoyed it, too. He was sure of it. She'd made a sexy little moaning sound in her throat and softened her mouth under his, granting him access to go deep, to stroke his tongue in and taste her...which had been his undoing.

Because now that he knew how sweet she was, his tastebuds cried out for more.

And his body ached. *Wanted*. Wanted what he shouldn't have.

Biting back another curse, he shut his laptop and stood up from his desk. He'd stared at the same col-umns and rows of figures for over an hour. Clearly work wasn't going to provide the distraction he'd hoped for.

He moved through the open French doors of his study and stood on the terrace, hands shoved in his jeans pockets, his gaze drifting out across the ocean to where the sun's glow was no more than a dying ember on the horizon.

It wasn't only the kiss that had played endlessly on his mind these last few hours. It was everything that had happened today. The village. The Gonzalezes. The stories about Camila Sanchez that he'd listened to over lunch...

The harsh things he'd said to Jordan in the car after-wards, which he now regretted.

Returning here, to the unapologetically plush sur-roundings of his home, had evoked in him a raft of strange emotions. He wasn't an idle man—he worked hard and always would—but there was no disputing the fact that his life had been one of privilege and opportunity. A life he'd have been denied had his birth mother chosen to keep him.

He lived the life of an aristocrat. He bore the de la Vega name. He sat on the Vega Corporation's board, owned a slice of the empire and held the position of Chief Executive—a role coveted by certain members of the extended de la Vega clan who believed it wasn't his birthright.

And they weren't wrong.

Dios. Wouldn't his father's cousin Hector and his son Diego just love to know that Xav had been born the illegitimate son of a farmer's daughter?

The sound of splashing water filtered into his thoughts and he found himself sauntering along the stone terrace and around the corner of the villa to where the swimming pool was located. He neared the water, saw a flash of long, pale limbs and froze, realising too late his mistake.

There was only one person—one *woman*—who'd be swimming in his pool.

He turned to leave.

'Xavier!'

Her soft voice curled through his insides like the silky song of a siren, sweet and seductive and impossible to resist.

'Would you hand me my towel, please?'

Damn it.

He turned back, saw the fluffy white towel on the lounger next to him and grabbed it just as she hoisted herself out of the water. Extending his arm so he didn't have to get too close, he held the towel out. But she didn't take it straight away, instead lifting her arms to wring out her hair.

Jaw clenched, he tried looking anywhere but at her. *Impossible*. Especially once he'd caught an eyeful of pert breasts and budded nipples under the wet, clingy Lycra of her crimson bikini top.

'For God's sake, Jordan,' he gritted out, before his self-control caved in and he let his gaze sweep the rest of her. 'Take the damn towel.'

Her eyes widened, and then her mouth pursed and she snatched the towel from him, wrapping it sarong-style around herself.

'You've had four hours to cool off,' she muttered. 'Don't tell me you're *still* angry.'

Angry? He almost laughed. Try deeply sexually frustrated. Or how about conflicted?

Because it was an unfamiliar kind of hell he found himself in—desiring a woman he shouldn't have. A woman who wasn't remotely suitable for him.

Over the past decade he'd been judicious in his choice of lovers. Not only because he'd felt the need to counterbalance his brother's playboy antics but because as Chief Executive he held himself to a higher standard. To command respect his behaviour had to be beyond reproach—not only in his professional life but his personal life as well.

Always there'd be those like Hector and Diego, hovering in the wings, watching and waiting for him to screw up, to prove himself unfit for the role.

As a rule he kept his relationships low-key and avoided one-night stands. He chose lovers who were emotionally mature and discreet about their personal lives, and he demanded exclusivity for the duration of their relationship, whether that be for two months or two years.

And he never, *never*, made himself vulnerable the way he had with Natasha.

When he'd hit thirty and succeeded his father as CEO he'd felt more keenly than ever the external pressure to 'settle down'. Many of his peers had taken wives, started producing the requisite heirs to their personal fortunes and empires. Conservative board members and shareholders preferred a leader who represented stability and family values. Hell, even his own brother had traded in his hedonistic lifestyle for the domestic idyll of marriage and fatherhood, giving their delighted parents their first grandchild—a baby girl—a few months ago.

Consequently Xav had become even more circumspect in his choice of lovers, narrowing his criteria to exclude women who didn't have the qualities of a desirable marriage partner.

The problem was that most women clung to the flawed romantic ideal of marrying for love, and he was too brutally honest to let a woman believe he would ever love her.

Respect, physical gratification, even affection…he could do all of these things. But love? With all its pressure and expectation and potential for pain? No.

Unfortunately that made finding the perfect woman damn near impossible. Which was why he had recently engaged the services of an exclusive high-end matchmaker—the very idea of which had drawn the patent disapproval of the woman standing before him now. A woman who'd also appeared scandalised at the idea of marrying for compatibility and not love.

And right there was all the deterrent he should need—without even going near the mind-bending fact that she was his birth mother's stepdaughter—and yet here he stood, mesmerised by a pair of golden-green eyes, a supple body and a lush mouth that made his own water hungrily at the recollection of driving her soft lips apart and delving into the honeyed depths—

'Xavier?'

His name was no more than a husky whisper across those beautiful lips, but it snapped him back to full consciousness. His palms felt cool and damp, and he saw with a jolt that his hands were curled over Jordan's wet shoulders. And he was close. So close their thighs and torsos almost touched. Her head tipped back on her slender neck to look up at him. Her eyes were big and round, lips parted.

Dios.

He didn't even remember moving. He jerked his hands off her body, stepped back, but she came with him and he realised one of her slim hands gripped the front of his polo shirt.

'Xavier, please… You've barely said a word to me since…'

She trailed off and he read frustration and confusion in her flushed face, but also desire. It was there in her widened pupils and her softly parted lips. In the way the hectic colour spilled down her throat and décolletage and stained the pale upper slopes of her breasts.

If he chose to do so right now he could carry her up to his room, peel away the wet bikini and satisfy his desire to taste her until she came against his tongue, and she wouldn't stop him.

The deeply erotic thought had him hardening and lengthening in his jeans until the tight fit of the denim was almost unbearable.

Never before had his self-control been so sorely tested...

'Jordan—'

'Don't.' A fierce look crossed her face. 'Don't say sorry. Or tell me you regret it. Because I don't.'

He heard the pride and defiance in her voice, and if he'd had any capacity whatsoever for gentleness just then he would have tried to spare her feelings. But the only way to keep a tight rein on his lust and prevent himself weakening was to be hard. Adamant.

'I do regret it,' he said, grasping her wrist and disentangling her fingers from his shirt. 'The kiss was a mistake.'

Hurt flashed in those big hazel eyes but her chin stayed boldly elevated. 'It didn't feel like a mistake to me. It felt pretty...amazing.'

He didn't like the way his pulse kicked then, as if his body agreed with her assessment.

'It *was* a mistake,' he repeated. 'And it won't happen again.' He released her wrist and stepped back. 'Goodnight, Jordan.' And he stalked back to his study.

CHAPTER SIX

JORDAN WOKE IN the morning feeling as mortified as she had when she'd crawled into bed last night.

She stared at the canopy above her head and pressed her palms to her cheeks. Just thinking about what had happened by the pool—or rather what *hadn't* happened—made her face burn and her stomach shrink all over again.

After hours of feeling as if her body was in the grip of a prolonged flush, she'd put her bikini on and slipped quietly out onto the terrace for an evening dip. She hadn't seen Xavier in hours. He had distanced himself as soon as they'd arrived at the villa, stalking off to his study and then letting her know via Rosa that he was working and wouldn't be joining her for a meal.

Jordan had filled the intervening hours with a bout of determined activity, taking a long walk down the tiered terraces to the private beach at the bottom of the property, then back up through the citrus orchards on the gentle slopes behind the villa.

On her return she'd followed her nose to the enormous kitchen, where the divine smells of fresh baking had wafted in the air. Rosa had fixed her a snack and then sat down and shared a pot of tea with her.

But nothing had distracted her completely from thoughts of *that* kiss.

Or, more disturbingly, from thoughts of what that kiss might have led to had they not been standing on a public street but somewhere more private.

As for what had possessed her to ask him to hand her the towel when she'd been perfectly able to fetch it herself… She only knew that her heart had leapt into her throat when she'd surfaced from under the water and spied him walking away. She'd called out his name on impulse, then quickly had to think of something to say.

He'd looked so attractive. Still in jeans, but with the white button-down shirt replaced by a black polo shirt that showed off his tanned, muscular arms and fitted snugly across his powerful shoulders and chest. His physique looked more like that of a professional athlete than a desk-bound executive. She'd wondered how a man who spent so much time in boardrooms and offices kept himself so lean and fit.

And then her ability to think anything at all had fled. His hands had come down on her shoulders and his expression had changed from annoyed to something much more intense.

He'd been going to kiss her again—she was sure of it—and her heart had raced, pumping a dizzying mix of desire and adrenaline into her bloodstream.

Without realising it she'd gripped the front of his shirt and tipped her face up. *Wanting* to be kissed. Wanting to experience the same heady rush of excitement and endorphins as when he had trapped her against the car with his hard body and claimed her mouth with deliciously brutal force.

But then he'd abruptly backed off and she'd made an

utter fool of herself, clinging to his shirt. Telling him she thought their kiss had been amazing.

Oh, *God*. Had she really said that?

She squeezed her eyes shut. Why, oh, why had she set herself up for such a humiliating rejection?

And yet… He hadn't been unaffected by their kiss, had he? As evidenced by his erection!

An erection he had shamelessly and shockingly made her aware of.

She groaned. She was mortified *and* confused.

She got up and opened the blinds and the French doors, breathing deeply as fresh air and bright sunlight flooded the room. The exquisite view from the balcony never failed to amaze her. For a moment she stood and drank in the vista, imprinting the vivid colours of the landscape and the bright blue sea into her memory.

She couldn't stay. Xavier's withdrawal had sent a clear message. If she remained she'd outstay her welcome, and she couldn't bear the thought of lingering where she wasn't wanted. Besides, she had planned to spend only six days tops in Barcelona. Time enough to sightsee, do the day trip to Camila's village and give the letter to Xavier.

Check, check and check.

She headed for the shower. It was almost nine o'clock. A very late time to get up for her, but she supposed that was what happened when you lay awake half the night with an erotic slideshow of illicit imaginings running through your head.

On the upside, Xavier had most probably left for work by now, and the idea of not having to face him brought a surge of cowardly relief. This way was best. She'd spare him the inevitable awkwardness and herself any further embarrassment. She'd leave him a nice thank-you note, plus the money he hadn't taken the other night for the hostel bill, and go on her way with a clear conscience.

When she went downstairs with her backpack Rosa looked startled, and then dismayed when she explained she was leaving. The housekeeper insisted she at least stay for a cooked breakfast and she gratefully accepted.

Sitting on a stool at the enormous granite-topped island while Rosa bustled around the kitchen, she took out her palm tablet and booked a ticket for the next sailing to Mallorca.

Rosa slid a fluffy, delicious-looking omelette in front of her, disappeared for a few minutes while she ate, and returned with the envelope she'd asked for earlier.

When her taxi arrived she pressed the envelope with her note and the money inside it into Rosa's hand. 'Please give this to Xavier.' She leaned in and hugged the older woman. 'Thank you so much for your hospitality, Rosa. I'm sorry I've missed Delmar and Alfonso. Please say goodbye to them for me.'

Only when she was in the taxi and nearing Barcelona's busy port did she acknowledge the hollow feeling in her chest. It was so similar to the feeling she'd had in the days after her dad died, and again after Camila passed, that she couldn't understand why it should accost her now—and so intensely.

On impulse she opened her tote bag and found the photo Maria had given her. Xavier and his biological father were so alike, with those lean, dark good looks, it made her heart clutch to see it.

It wasn't difficult to imagine how a young Camila might have fallen head over heels.

An ache pressed against her breastbone. She felt as if she was stealing something precious from Xavier by not showing him the photo. Not sharing what she knew of his birth father.

But she'd tried.

And he had made it clear—*very* clear—he wasn't interested.

Maybe down the track she would write to him from Australia. Explain what Maria had told her. Then he could decide whether to use the information or discard it.

The taxi pulled up outside the ferry terminal and Jordan put the photo away. The driver helped her retrieve her backpack, and then it took her a moment to sort out the right bills and coins to pay him.

Once he was happy she hoisted her pack onto her shoulder, turned towards the terminal—and slammed into a wall of solid muscle.

The impact combined with the weight of her pack threw her off-balance, and she stumbled backwards with a startled cry.

Strong hands caught her by the upper arms, stopping her from falling.

She looked up and her mouth dried.

'Xavier!'

'Running away, Jordan?'

She tried to focus on what he'd said instead of the heat of his hands, which felt like branding irons on her bare arms. 'Wh-what?'

In her peripheral vision a big, dark-suited man emerged from inside the terminal and strode towards them.

Juan.

He lifted his hand in the air and signalled to someone she couldn't see.

She turned her attention back to Xavier. His expression was inscrutable, but the hard glint in his gunmetal gaze told her he wasn't happy.

Her mind spun.

Rosa. Rosa must have called him. How else had he known she'd left? Where she'd gone?

Her voice was a croak of confusion. 'What are you doing here?'

'You left without saying goodbye.' His tone was mild, as though he'd dished out nothing more than a gentle rebuke, but she sensed the pull of a dangerous undercurrent in the air.

She sucked in her breath, ignored the stab in her belly that felt a bit like guilt. Did he really think she'd buy into the idea that *he* was the wounded party? If anyone had reason to feel slighted it was her. He'd invited her to his home under false pretences. He hadn't trusted her. He'd had her *investigated.* And then he'd messed with her in the cruellest way possible. He'd kissed her and left her wanting more, then rejected her and left her feeling like a fool. Humiliated.

She hiked up her chin. 'I left you a note.'

A muscle flickered in his cheek, and this time his voice was not so smooth. 'Do you think a *note* is the best way to finish things between us?'

Her heart thumped against her ribs. Finish things? What things? There wasn't anything *to* finish.

Was there…?

'Xavier—'

'Not here.' He dropped one hand, but kept the other on her arm, turning her away from the busy terminal.

A big black SUV pulled up to the kerb and she eyed it with a growing sense of *déjà vu*. Too fast for her to stop him, Juan took her tote bag from her hand and slipped the backpack off her shoulder.

Her heart lurched into her throat. 'Wait—stop.'

Both men ignored her. Xavier opened the rear door and she braced her palm against the top of the frame. Her initial shock was receding. In its place came agitation—and anger.

A shrill note entered her voice. 'I said *stop.*'

Xavier stilled. Then he released her arm, slid his hand around her waist and tugged her in close.

Anyone watching would have seen an intimate embrace, would have been unaware of the tension in the taut lines of his body beneath the tailored suit, or the tacit warning in the strong press of his fingers at her waist.

'I would prefer you didn't make a scene,' he murmured, and his mouth was so close to her ear she felt the warmth of his breath feather over her skin and caught his citrus and sandalwood scent.

Her senses reeled. It took all her strength to keep her knees locked so she didn't give in to temptation and lean into all that male hardness and heat.

She controlled her voice. 'I can't go with you.'

'Can't or won't?'

She glared. 'I need to check in for the ferry. I've already bought a ticket for the next sailing.'

'I'll buy you another one.'

She opened her mouth, but then a taxi driver honked his horn and gesticulated out of his window at the SUV, which idled in a drop-off only zone.

Juan yelled at the driver and the driver bellowed back. People started to look.

'Jordan,' Xavier urged, his mouth tightening, the fingers at her waist sinking deeper.

She flung her hands up. 'Fine! I'm getting in.'

And then she was going to tell him exactly what she thought of his arrogant, domineering behaviour.

Or at least she *would* have done, she assured herself ten seconds later, if he hadn't climbed in from the other side and at the same time pulled his ringing phone from his jacket and answered it.

She wanted to snatch the phone and throw the damned thing out the window.

Instead she bit her tongue while he conducted a conversation with someone else. Someone far more important than her, obviously. She folded her arms and focused on her anger as the car pulled away from the port.

She needed to stay mad.

If she stayed mad then maybe she could ignore this fluttery, breathless sensation in her chest that felt an awful lot like excitement.

Excitement?

Honestly. What was wrong with her? He'd virtually abducted her off the street. Again. The only thing she should be feeling was outrage.

He didn't end his call until they were descending into the basement of the Vega Tower, by which time her anger was a low simmer that rapidly changed to dismay and a faint sense of panic.

As soon as he'd slipped his phone back into his jacket she blurted, 'I can't go into your offices dressed like this!'

She could just picture the beautiful, flawless Lucia, looking at her in her denim cut-offs and tank top with barely concealed horror.

His gaze slid over her, settling briefly on her bare

thighs before lifting back to her face. For a second, as their gazes meshed and her breath snagged, she thought she saw a flash of heat in those metallic grey eyes before his features grew shuttered again.

'We're not going to my office.'

They went instead to the very top of the tower, via a dedicated lift that ran from the underground car park and gave access to two other levels: the forty-fourth floor, where the executive offices were located, and the floor above, which housed the corporate apartment that Rosa had mentioned as being where he sometimes stayed when he worked long hours.

The lift was one of those super-fast types that made her feel as if her stomach had relocated to her knees, and yet every second of the brief ride felt more like a minute, and every one of those was excruciating.

Because Xavier couldn't behave like an ordinary person and face the doors. No. He had to stand with his back to one of the side walls, so that no matter where Jordan stood she couldn't escape his incisive gaze.

As if she was going to perform some kind of Houdini act and disappear from under his nose while the lift was moving!

He stood tall and silent, his hands in his trouser pockets, her bags sitting on the floor beside him.

And he watched her.

She knew it—could feel his gaze like the stroke of a warm hand across bare skin even as she concentrated hard on the toes of her tennis shoes.

Coward. Look at him. Show him you're just as mad at him as he is at you.

And he *was* angry. She didn't need to sneak a look at the tight clench of his clean-shaven jaw to know it.

When irritated or frustrated he pinched the bridge of his nose, but when he was angry—truly angry—he simply went very, very still.

Like he was now.

It gave her a small shock to realise she knew all this about him. She'd known him for—what? Five days? Somehow it seemed longer.

So what? Stay mad, she reminded herself—an instruction she promptly forgot as she stepped from the lift straight into the expansive glass-walled living area of Xavier's penthouse apartment.

Wow.

It was nothing like the beautiful stone villa on the coast, but just as spectacular with its panoramic bird's-eye view of the sprawling city and the wide blue of the ocean beyond.

Automatically she moved to one of the floor-to-ceiling windows for a better look. From up here she could see the port in the distance and a number of berthed ships, one of which was probably the ferry that would have taken her away from here.

Away from him.

Away from this overwhelming attraction she didn't know how to handle and away from the danger of humiliating herself again.

She glanced at her watch. There was still over an hour until the ferry was scheduled to leave.

'Forget it, Jordan.'

She turned and frowned. 'Forget what?'

'You're not taking that ferry.'

It annoyed her immensely that he could read her thoughts as easily as she could read the idiosyncrasies of his body language.

She felt equally annoyed at how devastatingly gorgeous he looked, standing there in the middle of his living room in his dark grey suit, every bit as sleek and expensive-looking as the designer decor and stunning pieces of artwork that lined the interior walls.

She licked her lips, but there wasn't enough moisture in her mouth to alleviate their dryness.

'Why am I here?' she challenged, choosing to skip the more obvious *Why are you angry?*

She didn't need a psychology degree to work that out. Anyone who spent time with this man would see he had a penchant for control—and people who liked being in control didn't like surprises…unless *they* were doing the surprising.

She guessed her upping and leaving without saying goodbye in person had surprised him.

Throw a hefty dose of male ego and dented pride into the mix and you had all the ingredients for a grown man's temper tantrum.

So, yes. She wanted to know what he planned to do now.

Vent his anger?

Yell a bit?

Yell a *lot*?

She shook off any lingering cowardice and raised her chin, giving him a bold, defiant look.

Do your worst.

Because, really, how frightening could his worst be? She was a trauma nurse who'd worked the weekend night shift in Accident & Emergency. She had placated belligerent drug addicts. Fended off breast-and-buttgrabbing drunks. Had the unmentionable contents of a bedpan thrown at her…

A billionaire in a bad mood? *Pfft.* Child's play.

His eyes narrowed. And then *he* did something surprising and removed his suit jacket, shrugging his broad shoulders out of the expensive fabric and dropping the jacket onto the end of the long, coffee-coloured sofa behind him.

Jordan's eyes widened, but he didn't stop there. He upped the surprise factor another notch by lifting his hands to his throat, working his tie loose and sliding it out from under his collar.

Her breath shortened, and for one slightly hysterical moment she wondered if they were playing some kind of bizarre game of one-upmanship. Because when she thought about it they'd been surprising the hell out of each other from the moment she'd walked into his office last week and told him her late stepmom was his biological mother.

If she were keeping score she would have said before yesterday that they were level pegging. But then Xavier had stormed into the lead with that blistering, spine-loosening kiss she was trying very hard *not* to think about right now.

He threw the tie onto the sofa, then undid the button of his collar one-handed. His gaze stayed on hers, direct and unsettling, and she couldn't for the life of her look away.

'We have unfinished business.'

She swallowed, but her throat was dry and her voice came out husky. 'What business?'

He stalked across the plush carpet towards her and she stood like a deer in headlights, trapped by the silver snare of his gaze. On some deep, instinctive level she understood what was happening. Understood that beneath the ruthless self-control there wasn't only anger and ego railing against their restraints but something much more primal and volatile. Something that, if he chose to unleash it, neither of them would escape from unscathed.

And yet her conscious mind couldn't process it. Couldn't reconcile the hot, glittering intent in his eyes with the cold slap of his words from last night.

'It was a mistake—and it won't happen again.'

He stopped in front of her and she felt her pulse spike and her entire body tremble. But, even knowing what he intended, she couldn't make herself move. She felt as if she were in the grip of some sort of delirium—like a storm chaser standing in the path of a destructive tornado, torn between excitement and terror.

His hands came up and bracketed her head, his long fingers splaying into her hair. 'This business,' he said, his voice rough and deep. And Jordan had scarcely a second to snatch in her breath before his mouth rocked savagely over hers.

She didn't feign shock. Didn't make any token attempts to resist. The simple, irrefutable truth was that she'd yearned for him to do this, ached for him to touch her again, and denying it was like trying to hold back a storm.

Impossible.

She wanted to run *into* the storm. Wanted it to sweep her up and consume her in its chaos. Drown out the voice of sanity that would tell her all the reasons why they shouldn't do this.

His kiss wasn't gentle and she didn't want it to be. It was searing and fierce. Dominating and deep. He cradled her skull and prised her lips apart, driving heat and sensation into her mouth, demanding a response that she gave with a bold flick of her tongue against his.

She felt his tiny jerk of surprise, heard a small growl of what she hoped was approval in his throat, and then she was kissing him back, and it was wild and passionate. An urgent, breathless clash of lips and tongues unlike anything she'd experienced before.

Driven by instinct, and a feverish need for greater contact, she clung to his shoulders and arched against him, revelling in the delicious rub of hard male muscle against her softer curves.

When his strong hands curled under her buttocks and lifted her it seemed like the most natural thing in the world for her to wrap her legs around him and continue kissing him as he carried her effortlessly across the room.

He stopped at the sofa and she unhooked her ankles as he lowered himself to a seated position on the cushions, bringing her with him so that she sat astride him, her bare legs straddling his muscular thighs. The slightly rough landing bumped their mouths apart and she sat back, hands braced on his wide shoulders to steady herself, and looked at him.

His eyes glittered under heavy lids and dark colour slashed his cheekbones. Like her, he was breathing hard. *'Dios,'* he said, his voice little more than a harsh whisper. 'What spell have you cast over me, woman?'

His ragged words and the heat in his eyes sent a ripple of heady pleasure through her. To know that he felt as helplessly compelled by their attraction as she, that his desire for her pushed him to the limits of his control, made her feel sexually powerful and confident in a way she'd never felt before.

She licked her lips and leaned forward, eager to have his hot mouth on hers again. But he stopped her, putting his hands on her rib cage, tantalisingly close to her breasts.

He eased her back and said, 'I want to look at you,' and her flushed cheeks grew even hotter.

Reaching up a hand, he stroked the tip of his forefinger over her bottom lip, then trailed his fingers along her jaw, igniting a shower of sparks beneath her skin. Light as a feather, his touch continued down her throat, over the ridge of her collarbone and lower, eliciting a shiver of delight she couldn't suppress.

'Like silk,' he murmured, and then closed his hand over her left breast and squeezed in a way that was brazen and possessive and made her a gasp aloud. 'Take your hair down,' he commanded, and it didn't even occur to her to take exception to his tone. She was too far gone, too aroused, and for some reason the arrogant air of authority that normally rubbed her the wrong way only turned her on.

His hands had already played havoc with her ponytail, leaving it slightly askew, with long strands hanging loose about her face. She pulled the elastic band off and freed the rest, shaking her head until the wavy tresses tumbled over her shoulders and down her back.

Xavier lifted his hands and smoothed the hair back from her face, then drifted his long fingers through the silky ends and murmured something in Spanish. Voice husky, he reverted to English and said, 'Take off your top, Jordan.'

There was something deliciously risqué about his ordering her to strip for him. Before her confidence could waver, she pulled her tank top up and over her head and let it fall from her fingers, watching his eyes darken as they focused on her breasts, encased still in the cups of her cotton bra. She saw his jaw lock tight, as if he waged some fierce internal battle, and again she became aware of the power *she* wielded, even though he was the one issuing commands.

Emboldened by the knowledge that she could so easily drive him to the brink of his control, she removed her bra and at the same time rocked her hips forward so she rubbed intimately against the hard ridge of flesh inside his trousers.

He sucked in his breath, then hooked his arm around her waist and flipped her on her back on the sofa. 'Temptress,' he growled, looming above her, his eyes shimmering with hunger and the promise of retribution as he palmed one of her breasts and dragged his thumb over the extended nipple.

Sensation arrowed from her breast down to the place between her legs where she ached with need. She gasped and arched her back in a wordless plea for more—more than just that fleeting, teasing caress of his thumb—and a smile of sensual satisfaction curved his mouth.

It was an utterly masculine smile that said he knew exactly what she wanted from him, exactly what her straining body craved and needed, and the dark glitter in his eyes promised to deliver.

He leaned down, finally took possession of her mouth again, and his kiss was deep and scorching, dragging the air from her lungs and making that needy ache in her pelvis burn exquisitely hot and bright. She could have kissed like that for ever, lost in the midst of hunger and passion, all rational thought conveniently suspended.

When his mouth left hers she almost moaned in protest, until she realised his lips weren't going far—just to the edge of her jaw, then along to the soft skin beneath her earlobe and down the curve of her throat, pressing searing kisses to flushed, sensitive flesh that quivered in anticipation of each new touch, all the way to the tip of her breast.

Jordan caught her breath, knowing instinctively what he would do next, and yet still she wasn't fully prepared for the lightning-hot sensation of him capturing her nipple between his lips and sucking her deep into his mouth. Her body arched and she tunnelled her fingers into the soft, thick hair at the back of his head, crying out at the unbearable pleasure he inflicted, afraid this sweet torture on its own would make her come.

He lavished the same attention on her other breast before blazing a trail of fire with his mouth down to her navel, where his tongue circled and dipped in an erotic fashion before travelling lower.

The ache between Jordan's thighs became so intense, so consuming, that when she heard him say, 'Raise your hips,' she obeyed automatically, realising only once her shorts and knickers had hit the floor that he'd stripped her completely naked.

His big hands stroked up her inner thighs and then pushed them apart, opening her up to his unabashed scrutiny.

'Xavier…' His name fell from her lips on a breathless whisper, and she didn't know if it was plea or protest.

'*Perfección,*' he murmured, and her cheeks burned at being so explicitly exposed and studied.

Slowly he ran a fingertip down through her bright red curls and then delved deeper, finding the place where she was hot and wet and thrumming with need. He looked up, caught her gaze and held it captive as he pushed his finger inside her.

Instantly she felt her inner muscles tighten, responding needily to the deep, intimate caress. He slid a second finger in, stretching her a little wider, increasing the pleasure as he stroked into her, sliding deeper and finding just the right spot…

Oh, God.

Her body tremored, rushing towards climax even before he lowered his head and used the hot, velvet slide of his tongue to hurtle her over the edge.

It was the hottest, most intense orgasm she'd ever had, exhilarating and yet embarrassing at the same time, because she came so fast and hard she couldn't control herself. Couldn't hold back the loud moan that climbed her throat or stop the almost violent contortion of her body as the spasms of pleasure hurtled through her.

Mortified, she turned her flaming face into a pillow as Xavier rose from between her legs. How had she fooled herself into thinking even for a second that he wouldn't be in total control of this encounter? Of *her.*

He slid his hand under her cheek and turned her face towards him. She kept her eyes closed and he laughed softly.

'It's a little late for shyness, *amante.*'

She forced herself to look at him. 'You've still got all your clothes on,' she croaked, 'and I've already—' She threw her forearm over her eyes, unable to finish.

He eased her arm away and made her look at him again. 'The first of many,' he said, his voice a deep purr of promise that sent a delicious shiver down her spine.

His head lowered and her embarrassment receded

beneath a surge of anticipation as those sensual lips descended towards hers.

And then a loud chirruping sound came from the other end of the sofa and he tensed above her.

It took her a moment to realise it was his phone ringing.

He swore and started to draw away, and for a second she wanted to wrap her arms around his neck, pull him down to her and demand he not answer it.

He did answer it. Of course. And she saw his expression change as he listened, saw how after a minute he frowned down at her, naked and spreadeagled on the cushions, as if he were only just then noticing her and wondering why a naked woman was lying on his sofa.

Mortification flooded back. Along with a cold dose of sanity. Swiftly she sat up, covering her breasts with her arm while reaching with her other hand for her discarded clothing.

Xavier turned away, sparing her the indignity of having to dress in front of him. He was speaking now, in a rapid stream of Spanish, and his voice grew muted as he walked into another room.

Jordan dressed quickly—and then didn't know what to do with herself. Or what to *think* of herself, for that matter, after what had just happened.

She walked over to the window and took a couple of deep breaths.

Madness.

That was what it had felt like. Crazy and breathless and desperate, and well beyond anything she'd experienced.

Not that she had a ton of experience with men. Josh had been her one and only lover. They'd worked at the same hospital in Sydney, so she'd known him for several months before they dated and slept together. After several more months he'd suggested she move in with him and she had, believing for a time that he was *the one*.

Foolish her. Josh was already married—to his career. He didn't need a wife—just a woman who would stroke his ego and happily take a back seat to his ambition to become the best and most lauded cardiothoracic surgeon in the world.

Ellie, bless her, had helped her move her things out of his place, given her a great big sympathy hug and then told her she'd done the right thing 'dumping that arrogant jerk'.

Jordan blew out a heavy breath. Xavier had Josh beaten hands down in the arrogance department.

She closed her eyes and leaned her forehead against the glass.

Heaven help her.

CHAPTER SEVEN

XAV DROPPED HIS phone onto the dresser in the master suite and went through to the bathroom. He leaned over the basin on the marble vanity and sluiced his face in cold water, then grabbed a towel and scrubbed his skin dry.

What he desperately needed to do was douse his entire body in ice-cold water, but he didn't have time for a shower.

His brother was downstairs in his office. It had been Ramon on the phone.

Xav cursed. Ramon had told him days ago—*and* reminded him during their phone call yesterday—that he was bringing his wife, Emily, and their baby daughter, Katie, to Barcelona for a week. They'd agreed to have lunch today to discuss the Reynaud deal, among other things.

How the hell had he forgotten?

He braced his palms on the edge of the vanity unit and pulled in a shuddering breath.

His mind had been elsewhere—that was how he'd forgotten. Arriving at the office at seven a.m. after a restless night, he'd tried to focus on work and instead found his mind returning repeatedly to the events of yesterday. In particular his abrupt treatment of Jordan by the pool.

He'd seen the hurt in her eyes before he'd walked away. Hurt she hadn't deserved. He'd rejected her for the right reasons, but the way he'd gone about it had been harsh. Wrong.

And walking away from her, shutting himself in his study for the rest of the evening, hadn't stopped the incessant *wanting*.

He had only himself to blame. Yes, she had provoked him, flirting with that guy on the beach, shoving the brother thing in his face, knowing it would push his buttons, but he'd spent a lifetime training himself not to react impulsively to provocation.

But this time he had reacted.

He'd kissed her out of anger and an inability to subdue his desire. Then he'd punished *her* for it, shutting her out, speaking barely a word to her afterwards.

By mid-morning a tight knot of guilt had settled in his gut.

He prided himself on being a man of principle and strong moral character—better than those who would undermine him—and yet he couldn't view his behaviour yesterday with any sense of pride.

As for his behaviour today...

He clenched his jaw and stared down at his white-knuckled hands, reluctant to look at his reflection in the mirror for fear he would see not himself but some half-crazed Neanderthal he hardly recognised.

How the hell had he ended up doing what he'd just done out there on the sofa?

It had been the furthest thing from his mind when he'd picked up the phone and called Rosa.

His plan had been simple. As simple as he and Jordan sharing a polite, civilised meal that would allow him to claw back some self-respect and prove he wasn't the bastard she had every reason to believe him to be.

Above all he'd resolved to keep a lid on his lust and, if necessary, rebuff any of her advances.

Gently.

Except when he'd called his housekeeper to tell her he'd be home to dine with his guest this evening Rosa had promptly told him his guest was gone.

At first he'd thought she meant that Jordan had ventured out for the day, and for a second he'd regretted not having had the forethought to put a car and driver at her disposal.

But, no. Rosa had meant *gone* gone.

Not coming back gone.

For ever gone.

Shock had mingled with disbelief, making his stomach harden, his chest tighten.

And then the anger had come—swift and hot and all-encompassing.

She'd left.

Of course he'd known her time in Barcelona would be limited. But to leave without a word? Without so much as a goodbye?

He didn't think his heart had ever thundered with such ferocity in his chest.

During the trip to the ferry terminal his blood had pounded with increasing agitation.

He knew there was only one daytime sailing to Mallorca, the other being late in the evening, so his chance of intercepting her was good.

But what if Rosa had been wrong about Jordan's plans?

Fortunately Rosa had been right.

And when Jordan had climbed out of the taxi, just metres away from where he stood, the mix of triumph and relief he'd felt was like a shot of adrenaline straight to his heart.

Only then had he fully appreciated that he'd acted— yet again, where Jordan was concerned—entirely on impulse, and hadn't thought ahead to what he would do after he stopped her.

He pushed away from the vanity now, returned to the bedroom and looked for a fresh shirt and matching tie in the walk-in wardrobe.

The smart thing for him to have done after his call with Rosa would have been to shrug his shoulders. Let Jordan go. But something about that woman fused his brain. Impelled him to make rash decisions. And, just like on Saturday, every instinct in him had railed against her leaving.

He unbuttoned his shirt and yanked it off, caught the scent of jasmine on the fabric and something earthier, muskier. He swallowed hard.

Truthfully he'd not had sex on his mind when he'd brought her up here, but he *had* struggled to harness his anger, even as a voice in his head had urged him to consider that his behaviour yesterday had given Jordan a perfectly valid reason to flee.

Perversely, that thinking had only made his mood deteriorate and his temper spike—because then he'd been angry not only at her but at himself.

Wrap all that in an atmosphere charged with sexual tension and sparks had been inevitable.

He buttoned up the fresh shirt, pinned gold cufflinks at his wrists, then grabbed the tie.

Jordan had lit the fuse. Hoisting her chin like she had, pursing her lush lips in a tight moue and throwing him that look of defiance…of pure, unadulterated challenge…

A man of principle he might be, but he was only mortal. And mortal men had limits.

Desires.

He scowled at his reflection in the mirror as he checked the knot of his tie was straight.

He'd never had a problem controlling his physical urges. His baser instincts. But he'd lost himself out there. Utterly. Completely.

Lost himself in *her.*

He smoothed his hair, where Jordan's hands had messed it up, then turned from his reflection with a sneer of self-disgust.

He'd been rough at first, kissing her like a lusting barbarian with no self-control and no knowledge of how a man should treat a woman.

She should have slapped him. Instead she'd arched those beautiful supple curves against him and kissed him back with an equal fire and, he'd sensed, a little anger of her own.

But he'd also sensed an honesty in her response. A refusal to play coy. There might have been an edge of savagery to their kiss, but it had also been raw and real, unlike anything he'd experienced before.

He had no doubt that if Ramon hadn't called he'd be buried deep inside her right now, oblivious to the fact that it was the middle of a work day and his secretary had no clue where he was. And to think he'd almost ignored his phone. Thank God he hadn't. His brother was one of the few people who knew the code to his apartment. Ramon could have walked in at any moment.

It was only that knowledge that had forced Xav to turn his back on Jordan and walk away. Because one glance at her lying naked on his sofa, hair tousled, lips swollen from his kisses and her skin still flushed from her stunningly sensual climax, and he'd wanted to throw down the phone and resume where they'd left off, regardless of the risk.

He slid his phone into his pocket. He had told Ramon to wait for him in his office and he needed to get down there. Before his brother—and his secretary—grew suspicious about his whereabouts.

As for Jordan… The idea he'd entertained of playing the perfect gentleman over a polite, civilised dinner now sounded more like an evening of agonising torture.

The truth was they'd gone beyond polite—way beyond—and there was no going back.

What he *did* need to get back was his focus and his concentration on work—something that had been woefully lacking in recent days.

With his body still in a state of semi-hardened arousal and his thoughts consumed by a certain redhead, however, he knew there was only one way to make that happen. And that was to finish what he'd started on his sofa.

Jordan heard movement behind her and turned from the window.

Xavier was off the phone. He wore a fresh shirt and matching tie, and she noticed he'd smoothed his hair.

It looked so perfect her fingers itched with a crazy urge to muss it up again.

He grabbed his suit jacket and put it on, and disappointment flared even though she'd already assumed they wouldn't pick up where they'd left off.

He came towards her and her treacherous body prickled with heat. He looked suave and imperturbable again—as if ten short minutes ago he hadn't had his face buried between her legs.

Her face flamed and she cursed mentally. She needed to control her thoughts. As Xavier seemed able to do. He'd obviously had no trouble diverting his mind from sex. Why did men compartmentalise so much better than women?

He kept coming and her pulse stumbled. Had there not been a wall of glass behind her she would have stepped backwards. She crossed her arms instead.

He slipped one hand around her waist.

Her eyes widened.

Then he raised her chin with his fingers and she blinked up at him—right before he planted a soft, lingering kiss on her mouth.

Her breath was bottled in her throat. Who would have thought the lips that before had scorched and devoured and subjugated could be so...*gentle*?

By the time his head lifted her knees had developed a serious wobble.

His gaze held hers. 'Forgive me, but I must return to the office.'

Afraid her hands might roam where they shouldn't if she freed them, she kept her arms folded, which provided the added benefit of a safety barrier between his chest and her breasts.

Blast him, she thought churlishly. Why couldn't he have said something arrogant and infuriating? Arrogant and infuriating she could deal with. But tender and apologetic...?

Not fair.

She turned her head to stare out of the window, because looking at the chiselled perfection of his face was not helping her to think straight. 'Am I supposed to sit here and wait for you? Because if we're done here I could still make that ferry sailing.'

He brought her chin back around, forcing her to look at him. '"Done"?' His grey eyes gleamed. 'I think we're a long way from done—' the hand on her back tugged her closer and she gasped at the feel of his erection through their clothing '—don't you?'

Heat singed her cheeks. And other parts of her anatomy.

She scowled. 'You said it was a mistake...kissing me,' she reminded him. 'You said it wouldn't happen again.'

He looked unconcerned. 'I was wrong. It happens once in a while,' he added, so deadpan she thought he was serious—until she saw the infinitesimal twitch at the corner of his mouth.

Her heart knocked against her ribs at this unexpected glimpse of teasing humour. It wasn't the first evidence she'd seen of a lighter side to Xavier, but coming now, on the heels of their intense sexual encounter, it threw her.

Was that his intent? To keep her off-balance? As a way to maintain the upper hand? Or was she being oversensitive now?

Drawing in a deep breath, she changed tack. 'Am I a prisoner here?'

His eyes narrowed at that. His hand slid off her waist and she told herself she didn't regret the loss of physical contact.

He pulled his phone from his pocket. 'I'm texting you the code for the elevator,' he said, doing it as he spoke, 'so you can come and go via the car park with privacy. If you prefer to stay in, you can relax here and no one will disturb you. There's an outdoor terrace and a lap pool, and you'll find the kitchen is stocked with essentials.' He slid the phone back into his pocket and settled his gaze on her. 'The answer to your question is no, Jordan. You are not a prisoner.'

She bit her lip. Her head spun as her brain desperately tried to make sense of what was happening here. What it *meant*. He'd not said it in so many words, but by providing her with unfettered access to and from the apartment he'd also given her the freedom to walk out and not return—yet he'd made it clear he didn't want her to leave.

Why? So they could finish their *'unfinished business'*? Was this about sex? *Just* sex? And, if so, why was she not scandalised by the idea?

Because you want him.

She felt her face flush again. Frustrated, and more than a little confused, she tore her gaze from his and turned back to the window. She didn't do casual sex. And that was what sex with Xavier would be. How could it be anything else? They lived on different sides of the world. She was just a tourist in his country. And, geography aside, he wasn't someone she'd ever set her long-term sights on anyway. They'd already clashed over their differing views on love and marriage. Theirs would be a short, steamy affair—nothing more.

Perfect! That was what Ellie would have said if she was there. Oh, Jordan could just see her friend's startling blue eyes glittering with glee. *Do it*, she'd say. *Live a little. Life is short and unpredictable.*

As trauma nurses, they both knew just how unpredictable life could be. How quickly and unexpectedly a life could end or change irreversibly. Jordan had lost her dad and her stepmom within four years of each other, and they'd both gone before their time. They'd had twelve wonderful years together, but they should have had longer.

What would Camila have thought about the attraction between her stepdaughter and Xavier?

He was her *son.*

Jordan imagined Ellie would have a ready answer for that too: *So what? He's not your brother!*

And hadn't Xavier made that same point with devastating effect yesterday?

She rubbed her fingers over her forehead. A week ago she hadn't thought sexual chemistry was really a thing. Now she knew better. But why couldn't she have made the discovery with a different man?

Why *this* man?

Her temples started to throb.

Was this powerful, overwhelming attraction a purely physical thing? Was it only Xavier's sublime good looks and potent masculinity that drew her? Or was it something else? Was a part of her subconsciously looking for a deeper connection with him because he was a living, breathing link to Camila, whom she missed desperately?

Good grief. Now she was really overthinking things! She groaned inwardly.

Or maybe she groaned aloud, because in her peripheral vision she saw Xavier move, then felt his hands curl gently over her shoulders from behind.

His touch set her pulse racing, as always, and yet there was something oddly grounding in the warmth and strength of those big, capable hands and the sense of his solid body behind her.

She felt his breath stir her hair as he spoke.

'I'd like to spend more time with you, Jordan.'

She swallowed. Was that code for *I want us to have sex*? She didn't know. She'd never been in this sort of situation before. Was there an etiquette? If there was, Xavier would know. Didn't wealthy men change their women as frequently as they changed their suits?

There was a silence, and then she heard him sigh. His hands tightened a little on her shoulders, and his voice lowered to a deep husk.

'I want you, Jordan. I can't deny that—not after what just happened on that sofa. We have a powerful chemistry, and I don't believe you want to walk away from it any more than I do right now.'

His candour shocked her, and yet his willingness to offer up such blunt honesty spoke to something inside her. Lent her the courage to offer some plain-spoken words of her own.

She turned, dislodging his hands from her shoulders in the process, and looked up at him. 'You accused me of running away today, and I suppose I was, in a way. After last night, by the pool…' She hitched a shoulder. 'I was embarrassed—and confused. You kissed me, Xavier, and then you rejected me. How was I supposed to feel? I thought I was doing us both a favour by leaving. I didn't mean to offend you or to seem ungrateful.'

She took a breath. Even her neck and the tips of her ears burned now, so she knew her blush was scarlet. But she forced herself to continue.

'Last night you said kissing me had been a mistake and now you're saying you were wrong... So I think maybe...even though you didn't do it in the nicest way... you were trying to do the right thing last night and be honourable, because you thought doing anything else would be taking advantage of me...'

Oh, God. Was she making any sense? Or just making a fool of herself?

She gulped in another lungful of air. Her heart pounded so hard she could hear the blood rushing in her ears. 'But now that we've...'

She flapped her hand in the general direction of the sofa, and Xavier lifted an eyebrow.

'Been intimate?'

More precisely she'd been thinking he'd given her the most amazing orgasm of her life. She decided to keep that to herself. 'Yes, now that we've done that...' And now she really had to screw up her courage, because she'd never had a conversation quite like this in her life, and the enigmatic look on Xavier's face gave her no clue what he was thinking. 'You're right. I don't think I want to walk away just yet.'

Because she was pretty sure that what she'd be walking away from was wild, passionate sex the likes of which she'd never experienced before and might never experience again.

Ellie was right. Life was unpredictable. Short. And too often filled with suffering and pain. She'd seen people lose loved ones and her empathy was strong, because she herself was intimately acquainted with that kind of loss. Her dad had died unexpectedly. And then had come Camila's illness and eventual passing... Towards the end there'd been days with Camila that had been harrowing and heartbreaking. Even now there were days when she woke and her stomach felt knotted, her chest tight.

But the woman who had sat on Xavier's lap a short while ago, who'd loosened her hair and daringly removed her bra—that woman hadn't felt pain, or grief, or loneliness. She'd felt only pleasure and excitement and the heady, delicious thrill of anticipation.

For just a few short days Jordan wanted to feel that—and more.

Boldly, she held his gaze. 'I want you, too.'

'I want you, too.'

'Are you listening, *hermano*?'

Xav jerked his head up. 'What?'

Ramon eyed him across the meeting table in his office. 'Where is your head today?'

Xav sat forward, pushed aside the plate at his elbow and grabbed his pen. He and Ramon had decided on a working lunch in the office rather than in a restaurant, where discussing sensitive matters might be difficult.

Ramon lounged in a chair on the other side of the table. He'd rolled up his shirtsleeves, removed his tie and loosened his collar. Xav supposed he should be grateful his brother hadn't yet removed his shoes and propped his feet on the table.

'First you forget our lunch,' Ramon needled, 'and now you seem incapable of concentrating for more than five minutes at a time.'

Xav scowled. 'My concentration is fine.' *Liar.* 'What else have you heard about Lloyd Anders?'

'Nothing more than what I told you yesterday. He and Reynaud were spotted having lunch together last week in New York. And then Anders wined and dined Reynaud and his wife on Friday night.'

'At *our* Manhattan club?'

'*Sí.*'

Xav gritted his teeth. He and Lloyd Anders had been business rivals for years, with their respective companies often competing for the same acquisition. He should have known a prize like Reynaud Industries was too tempting for Anders to ignore. But to make his move at the eleventh hour, when Xav was so close to finalising a deal with Reynaud, and then to have the balls to entertain Peter Reynaud and his wife in one of the Vega Corporation's own clubs...

Xav put his pen down before he snapped it.

'Frankly, I'm surprised Reynaud would consider Anders as a potential suitor for the business,' Ramon said. 'Reynaud is conservative. Old school. He has a paternalistic leadership style. If his son hadn't gone into medicine and his daughter hadn't died of leukaemia he'd be passing the company on to his children, not selling.'

Xav paused in the act of pouring himself another coffee. 'Leukaemia?'

'*Sí.* Died in her late teens.' Ramon pushed his cup across the table for a refill, a frown settling between his brows. 'Must've been devastating.'

It wasn't the sort of observation Xav would have expected his brother to make. But, he conceded, Ramon had undergone a remarkable transformation in the past year. From careless playboy to husband and father. Of course he'd have some idea of how traumatic it must be to lose a child. At eighteen he'd got a girl pregnant and she'd miscarried the baby. Now he had a daughter he cherished and, Xav suspected, would protect with his life.

He set the coffee pot down, recognising the sharp tug in his gut for what it was.

Envy.

Growing up, Ramon had been impulsive and reckless while Xav had done everything right. He'd played by the rules, put work before pleasure, strived every day to be the perfect son and make their parents proud.

He'd thought he would be the first to marry and give their parents grandchildren.

Not that he begrudged his brother and sister-in-law their happiness. Nor did he resent the existence of baby Katie. She was a beautiful child who carried the de la Vega genes—something his own offspring would not, regrettably, be blessed with.

The thought gave him pause.

He had chosen ignorance when it came to his genetic heritage, but what if he had children who one day wanted to know from whom they were descended? Was it his right to deny his offspring that knowledge?

A chill brushed his neck.

Could he unwittingly pass on genetic disorders to his children?

Was leukaemia hereditary?

'Anders hardly represents the kind of traditional values Reynaud holds in high regard,' Ramon said. 'The guy's in his midforties and already has two ex-wives. His last mistress looked as if she was barely out of college.' Ramon smirked. 'And didn't a story surface during his second marriage of a *ménage à trois* with the maid?'

Xav shook his head. He had no interest in the sordid details of Anders's personal life. Xav took pains to avoid the tabloids—both reading them and being *in* them.

How did Reynaud view *him*? He kept his nose clean, but the fact remained he was thirty-five and unmarried. Most people assumed that wealthy bachelors led a lifestyle of indulgence and excess whether they actually did or not.

He did not.

And the redhead upstairs...?

Xav ignored the snide inner voice. Jordan was not an indulgence. She was a sudden distracting itch he needed to scratch so he could move on and re-establish some normality.

He checked the time on his phone and stood. 'I have another meeting. Are you staying here this afternoon?'

Ramon drained his coffee. 'For a couple more hours. Lucia has set me up in the spare office down the hall. I'll come in for a few hours each day this week.'

'Fine.' Xav gathered up his papers. 'You're staying at Mamá and Papá's?'

'Of course. They insisted. Emily's barely been able to prise Katie from Mamá's arms.'

Ramon got up and collected his own things.

'Don't forget the family lunch on Saturday. Mamá will be upset if you don't show.'

Xav cursed under his breath. Five days from now... Would he and Jordan have had their fill of each other by then?

'The apartment's undergoing some renovation work,'

he said, the lie sliding off his tongue with almost disturbing ease. 'Stay clear of it.'

The last thing he needed was Ramon stumbling across Jordan. How would that conversation go?

Brother—meet my late birth mother's stepdaughter. Yes, I'm sleeping with her.

Or at least he would be soon.

It was a thought that tested his concentration as he sat down with the heads of his commercial and legal teams.

That meeting went on for an hour. The next one forty-five minutes—thirty of which he spent in his head, replaying the little speech Jordan had delivered upstairs.

How many people did he know who were as straightforward and honest? Willing to speak their minds even when it discomfited them to do so?

She'd berated him for his behaviour, interpreted his actions with unsettling accuracy, and then baldly stated that she wanted him—all while blushing like an ingénue.

He'd never been so turned on listening to a woman talk.

And he'd never wanted a woman as desperately as he wanted Jordan Walsh.

CHAPTER EIGHT

HE'D TOLD HER he'd be back no later than six.

When he stepped into the elevator it was almost seven. He punched in the security code and felt his heart pound as if he'd taken the stairs instead—all the way from the basement.

Anticipation, he told himself.

Yet he'd be lying if he didn't acknowledge that his pumping blood also fed a small vein of disquietude.

When Lucia had put a call through from one of the directors right on six o'clock he'd sent a brief text to Jordan advising her that he'd been waylaid.

He'd received no response.

What if, even after her blushing confession about wanting him, she'd changed her mind and fled?

The very thought sent a vicious twist of reaction through his stomach. He'd want to go after her, but he wouldn't. He'd barely been able to rationalise his actions the first time. If he chased her down again he'd look like a madman.

He stepped out of the elevator and scanned the large open-plan living space.

Her bags were gone.

His hands curled into fists.

No. *No.*

'Jordan?'

He checked the kitchen, found it empty, and was about to turn and stride out when his gaze caught on a bowl filled with a bright assortment of fruit on one of the black granite surfaces.

The tension in his muscles eased a bit. The bowl hadn't been there earlier. How likely was it that Jordan had decided to leave him a parting gift of fruit?

Quickening his pace, he headed towards the bedrooms, and there, in the smallest of the rooms, were her rucksack and handbag.

Mildly amused, he grabbed the bags and took them to the master bedroom. Did she think he would let her sleep in a separate room? He wasn't the kind of man who took his pleasure with a woman and then slept alone. When he took a lover to his bed he expected to find her next to him in the morning, preferably with a smile on her face and a body that was soft and willing.

He returned to the living room and spotted what he'd missed earlier—the large sliding door to the terrace sitting slightly ajar. He still couldn't see her, though—not until he went outside and saw she'd dragged one of the loungers into a shaded back corner of the terrace to escape the sun.

Was she sleeping?

He approached quietly. She lay on her side, her long legs curled up, her cheek resting on the back of one hand. Her hair flowed loose and he marvelled at the melding shades of red and copper and gold that never failed to fascinate him.

A paperback lay on the ground, a cardboard bookmark next to it. The haphazard placement of each suggested the book might have slipped from her grasp when she'd nodded off.

Would she be annoyed when she woke to find she'd lost her place?

He found his mouth curving as he pictured that little scowl she developed when she was unhappy about something—the one that made her look about as fearsome as a grumpy kitten with its hackles up.

He'd seen that expression a number of times in the last five days—usually when she was making her dissatisfaction with his behaviour known.

It occurred to him there was no one in his life who dared to call him out on his arrogance the way she did—except maybe for his mother, who did so only occasionally and was wise enough to know when to give his temper a wide berth.

He crouched beside the lounger, unable to resist tucking a stray copper curl behind her ear. Her nose was still pink from yesterday, and he was pleased she'd sought the shade to protect her skin.

She stirred, her soft lips parting, but her eyes stayed closed. She whispered something and he leaned in to catch the words.

'Is she coming back?'

He realised she was still asleep, or maybe hovering in that place between sleep and wakefulness where dreams and reality sometimes blurred.

Had she meant Camila?

His heartbeat slowed as he thought back to that first meeting in his office.

Six weeks. Wasn't that how long she'd said it had been since her stepmother had died?

It wasn't long.

A sudden surge of tenderness took the edge off the potent, ever-present desire that hummed inside him like an electric current when he was around her.

Jordan projected such natural buoyancy and strength it was easy to forget she must still be grieving. Hurting.

His chest tightened and for a moment he had a strange sense that he shared in her loss. That somehow Camila's passing had forged a bond between himself and Jordan— a connection that ran deeper than sexual attraction.

As swiftly as the feeling overtook him, however, he shook it off. How could he grieve for a woman he'd never known?

He leaned in again and spoke softly. 'No, *querida*. She's gone. But I'm here.'

He scooped her into his arms and stood, and she murmured some unintelligible words and burrowed her face into his neck.

In the master suite he lowered her onto the bed, his brain waging a fierce battle with his body. One urged him to tuck a blanket around her and walk away. The other wanted to undress her and explore every inch of her luscious body.

He started to straighten, but her arms tightened around his neck.

'Xavier?'

He looked down, straight into those extraordinary golden-green eyes, wide open now, staring up at him, searching his.

'Where are you going?' Her voice was deliciously husky. 'I've been waiting for you.'

It was all the invitation he needed. Planting his hands either side of her head, he lowered himself to the bed and settled his mouth over hers.

She opened to him immediately, and he almost groaned at the feel of her plump lips softening and parting under his.

For seven hours he'd thought about doing this. Seven hours of struggling to concentrate through meetings and phone calls and the usual endless influx of emails and papers crossing his desk, all demanding his time and attention.

He cupped her jaw in one hand, holding her still so he could explore the contours of her mouth with his lips and tongue, forcing himself to take a gentler, more leisurely approach than he had previously.

He intended to have her as many times as he desired—as many times as was necessary for his lust to burn itself out—but he didn't want their first time to be a rushed, frantic coupling. He wanted to savour her, inch by exquisite inch, to prolong the experience and wring every drop of pleasure from it—for him and for her.

The problem was, while frustration and anger weren't driving him now, his hunger for her felt no less urgent and raw. Thirty seconds of kissing and already he was having to restrain himself.

He angled his head and took the kiss deeper, dipping his tongue in, enjoying the way hers came out to duel and dance with his, her strokes and thrusts growing bolder by the second.

He felt her hands slide to the back of his head, her fingers clutching at his hair, and then she sucked his bottom lip into her mouth, the mischievous nip of her teeth shooting a dart of heat straight to the base of his groin.

Now he did groan—a deep, masculine sound of appreciation that rumbled up his throat.

She was honey and temptation—sugar and sin—mixed together in one soft, seductive package.

He felt sweat film his brow just as Jordan tugged on his tie and whispered against his lips.

'You're overdressed.'

Yes—and hot as hell. But to undress he would have to stop kissing her.

Instead he yanked his tie loose, managed to shrug one shoulder out of his jacket, but finally frustration—and the desire to feel nothing but heat and sweat between their bodies—forced him to raise his head.

'Don't move,' he growled.

He shed his clothes, snapping a few buttons off his shirt and losing his cufflinks on the floor in his haste. Jordan was up on her elbows, watching, her eyes growing wider with each item of clothing he removed.

When he pushed his boxers down and kicked them off, freeing the long, heavy shaft of his erection, her teeth sank into her bottom lip and her thick copper lashes swept down and shielded her eyes from view.

He crossed back to the bed, leaned down and took her face in his hands, and kissed her, long and slow, before easing back.

'Lift your arms,' he ordered, desire roughening his voice, and she did so, allowing him to pull her top up and over her head.

With deft hands he stripped away the rest of her clothing until she lay completely naked on the bed, and for a moment his breathing stopped as he feasted his hungry gaze on the long, graceful lines and lush curves of her body.

A pink blush spilled down her neck, belated shyness making her move to cover herself.

'No.' He caught her wrists and pulled her arms above her head. 'You're beautiful.'

And then he came down onto the bed and lost himself in a thorough, sensual exploration of her body. Her pleasure, he quickly discovered, intensified his, and he let her responses guide him, paying close attention to her soft gasps and delightful moans, to the little telltale shivers that rippled through her body.

One by one he found her pleasure spots. By the time he trailed kisses along her smooth inner thighs he knew she was close to the edge.

Remembering how he'd made her climax on the sofa, he used his hands and mouth in the same way now, and within seconds her spine arched and she cried out and came in a beautiful, shuddering rush.

Heat ripped through his body, and in that moment he knew that watching Jordan in the contorted throes of orgasm was the single most erotic experience of his life.

He sheathed himself with a condom and noticed that his hands shook.

'Xavier...' Her voice was husky, plaintive, and he moved over her, covering her body with his.

'I'm here, *amante*.'

Her hands stroked over the muscles of his shoulders and back and down to his buttocks, drawing him to her as he positioned himself between her spread legs. Their gazes meshed for a moment, then he drove his hips forward and they both gasped as he thrust himself deep inside her.

His breath shuddered out of him, and then Jordan raised her knees and tilted her pelvis, causing friction, and he hurriedly sank his fingers into her hip.

'Wait,' he rasped, teeth gritted, needing a moment to rein himself in.

He closed his eyes. She was so hot. So tight. He felt her flesh stretch to accommodate his considerable width, then contract again, gripping him along every sensitised inch of his shaft.

'Xavier?'

He opened his eyes, saw uncertainty and concern on her beautiful, flushed face.

She reached up and lightly touched his clenched jaw. 'Is…is everything all right?'

He relaxed his expression. *'Sí, querida,'* he said, his voice hoarse. 'Everything is perfect.' He smoothed her hair back from her forehead and kissed her on the mouth. 'You're perfect.'

He moved and felt the tight, greedy clench of her internal muscles as he slowly drew out and then, at the last possible moment, plunged back in. The sensations were exquisite, torturous.

The slow, steady rhythm he'd intended to set to coax her towards climax again lasted all of five seconds.

He couldn't hold back. His body screamed for release. Demanded that he *take*. With a low groan of surrender he gave himself over to the dark, animalistic urges inside him and let go, each thrust harder, deeper than the last.

Jordan wound her arms around his neck, raised her mouth to his ear and whispered something shockingly dirty that drove him over the edge.

And then there was nothing but a streak of white-hot sensation and the rough, savage sound that ripped from his throat.

* * *

It took Jordan a long while to float back to earth. For a time she wondered how all the tiny scattered pieces of her could possibly reassemble themselves so that she looked and felt the same as before—and then she decided they wouldn't.

It wasn't possible.

After that mind-blowing, body-shattering experience she would never be the same again.

She would certainly never look at sex in the same light. Because now she knew. Knew that what she'd experienced with Josh had been a pale imitation of what true unbridled passion looked like. That sex with a man who elevated her pleasure above his, who knew where to find every erogenous zone on her body and how to make her feel worshipped and desired, was a thrilling experience every heterosexual woman should have at least once in her life.

Not that Jordan could imagine once being enough.

Not even close.

'What are you thinking?'

The deep rumble of Xavier's voice penetrated her thoughts. Without lifting her cheek off his shoulder she tilted her face to his. She lay in the circle of his arms, tucked against his side, her forearm draped over washboard abs so impressive she'd already promised herself she'd eat less chocolate and do sit-ups every morning.

Or maybe just sit-ups, she amended. Life was too short to deny herself chocolate.

Or wild, exhilarating sex...

'Jordan?' His arms tightened around her and his large hand stroked up and down her arm.

She felt her heart thud unevenly. She reminded herself she mustn't enjoy this part too much. They'd had amazing sex, but she would not build it into something it wasn't in her head. Her rose-tinted glasses would remain firmly under lock and key.

But a little post-coital euphoria wouldn't do her any harm. Besides, how could she pretend that being cocooned in these big, strong arms was anything less than bliss? Not to mention a surprise. Who would have pegged the formidable Xavier de la Vega as a cuddler?

Smiling to herself, she tucked her chin back down and let her gaze drift across his hair-roughened chest. 'What was the question again?'

'What are you thinking about?'

She was thinking he had ruined her future sex-life, because no other man would ever compare. 'I reserve the right not to answer that question.'

'On what grounds?'

'On the grounds that my answer may go to your head.'

'Which head?'

She was slow to register his meaning. Then a snigger escaped her. 'I can't believe you said that.'

'Says the woman who asked me to f—'

She jerked up and slapped her fingers over his mouth. 'That's different,' she defended, colour singeing her cheeks. 'That was in the heat of the moment.'

And the heat in that particular moment had been blistering—so intense Jordan had half expected the sheets to ignite and engulf them both in flames.

She'd sensed the change in Xavier, known the exact moment his prized control slipped from his grasp. Had he been another man, his sheer size and the power of his body as he surged between her legs might have made her feel vulnerable, but she trusted Xavier, and instead of fear she'd felt a thrill of wild excitement. His control had been in tatters because of *her*, and that intoxicating knowledge had made her brazen. Daring.

He grabbed her wrist and tugged so she ended up sprawled over his chest. Her pulse quickened. The light abrasion of chest hair against her sensitive breasts was far too tantalising.

His grey eyes gleamed. 'I never would have picked you for a dirty talker, Ms Walsh.'

Neither would she. But then she wouldn't have picked herself for a one-night stand kind of girl, either.

The thought was unwelcome and sobering. A reminder that this—whatever 'this' was, exactly—was temporary. Just how temporary she hadn't yet worked out. For all she knew Xavier could be intending on taking her back to the ferry terminal tomorrow. Maybe for him once was enough.

A tiny sliver of ice pierced her euphoria.

Quickly she rolled away, managing to reach the side of the bed before a strong arm looped around her waist and hauled her back against a hot, muscular body.

Xavier growled in her ear. 'Where do you think you're going?'

Treacherous heat poured through her. 'I—I put my things in one of the other bedrooms.'

She hadn't wanted to make any assumptions about where she'd sleep—and she was glad now that she hadn't. It gave her an excuse to vacate his bed without suffering the humiliation of being asked to leave. The cuddling had been nice, but just because he held her in the immediate aftermath of lovemaking it didn't mean he wanted her in his bed all night.

'I moved your things. They're here…in the dressing room.'

'Oh.' And now she felt foolish.

'Do you have a problem with sleeping in my bed, Jordan?' His voice was dark and velvety, with the tiniest hint of menace.

'No. I just…' She tried for a careless shrug. 'I don't know what the rules are, that's all…' Her face burned. 'I don't usually do this sort of thing.'

With a manoeuvre that left her startled and breathless, he flipped her on her back and loomed above her. '"This sort of thing"?'

She swallowed. 'Casual sex.'

He made a low, rough sound. 'I'm pleased to hear it.'

Pleased to hear what? That she was nowhere near as experienced as him? She wished she'd said something different. Something that would have portrayed her as a woman of the world. The type of woman who could blithely indulge in a sexual fling and walk away without a backward glance.

He circled her left nipple with his fingertip. 'There's only one rule you need to know, *amante*.'

She tried to ignore the little ring of fire his finger created. 'What does that mean?'

'What?'

'Amante?'

His lips curved in a smile that was altogether too sexy. A smile that made her body heat and her insides melt. The heat was welcome, but not the melting. The melting of organs—especially the one in her chest—was strictly forbidden.

'Lover,' he said, and then dipped his head and drew her nipple into his mouth.

Oh, God.

She fought to concentrate. 'And—' She gasped as he sucked harder. 'Wh-what's the rule?'

After several more seconds of inflicting sweet torture on her he lifted his head and locked his glittering gaze onto hers. 'You don't walk away from this—from *me*—until we've burned it out.'

Which meant he believed their attraction had a shelf life. Was that how it was with this kind of crazy, intense chemistry? Did the passion flare hot and bright for a brief time and then naturally extinguish itself?

She didn't know if she found the idea reassuring or depressing.

His hand trailed over her stomach and she lost her train of thought. Tiny tremors of anticipation quaked through her. His mouth descended towards hers.

And then a grumbling noise, horribly loud and endlessly long, filled the air.

Jordan froze.

Xavier lifted his head and looked at her. 'Was that your stomach?'

Wishing she could disappear, she covered her face with her hands. 'Yes!' She glared at him through her fingers. 'Are you laughing at me?'

He was. Which meant she had not only his sexy smile to contend with, but the rich, delicious sound of his low laughter.

He straightened, took her hands and pulled her into a sitting position.

She gave him a look of dismay. 'What are you doing?'

'*We* are getting up,' he said. 'And then I'm ordering some food.'

She dropped her gaze to the very impressive semierect appendage between his legs. She raised an eyebrow. 'Wouldn't you rather do something else?' *She* would.

'*Sí*. But you need to eat.'

'I'm not hungry.'

He tipped up her chin. 'That's a lie. We both need to eat. And believe me, *amante*—' his sudden smile was wolfish '—you'll need the energy for the night ahead.'

If watching Jordan climax was at the top of his list of most erotic experiences, then watching her devour half a dozen raw oysters came a close second.

She picked up another shell. 'These are *so* good. Aren't you having any?'

She angled the shell, swallowed the oyster down and closed her eyes, savouring the taste on her tongue for a moment before tipping her head back and letting the fish slide down her delicate throat.

Xav shifted on his chair, grateful they were seated at his dining table in the open-plan living area. The tabletop hid what his sweatpants most definitely did not.

'I can take or leave shellfish.'

'You don't mind if I have the last one?'

He flourished a hand. 'Be my guest.'

She made short work of the last oyster, wiped her mouth on a napkin and took a sip of her white wine. Her gaze moved over the selection of tapas dishes spread across the table. 'This is fancy for takeout.'

'It's from a local restaurant.'

'And they deliver?'

'They do for me.'

She pulled one of the plates closer, eyeing the deep-fried balls of potato and minced meat drizzled with aioli and spicy sauce. 'I think I know these—they're *bombas*, aren't they?'

'*Sí*. You've had them before?'

She nodded. 'My first night here. I went for a wander through the city and ended up eating at a small tapas bar.' She picked up her fork. 'I remember these were delicious.'

He frowned. 'Alone?'

She finished her mouthful. 'Yum! Even better than the ones I had before. Yes.' She glanced up at him. 'Alone.'

The thought of her walking the city streets at night unaccompanied sent an icy trickle down his spine. 'Why do this trip on your own?' he asked abruptly. 'Don't you have someone who would have travelled with you?'

She shrugged. 'My friends are working. And if one of them had taken some leave to come with me it would have meant a more disciplined timeframe and itinerary. I don't have a job waiting for me, and travelling by myself gives me flexibility. If I want to spend a few extra nights somewhere, or change the order of places I visit, I can.'

He couched his next question in a more casual tone. 'How much time did you plan to spend in Spain?'

She pushed her hair out of her face. 'About three and a half weeks. I plan to travel for about a month altogether, but I want to do a few days in London on my way back.'

'Why London?'

Another shrug. 'It's on my list. I've always wanted to see *Les Misérables* in the West End.'

'You have a list?'

She broke off another chunk of *bomba*. 'I have two

lists. A "must" list and an "if there's time" list. Both include places to see and things to do.'

He sipped his wine. 'What else is on your "must" list?'

She swallowed her food. 'Mallorca,' she said with a pointed glance. No doubt to emphasise that Mallorca was where she'd be now, if not for him.

Xav sent back a smouldering look to remind her she hadn't complained about that an hour ago, when she'd been naked and underneath him.

Her face turned pink and she cleared her throat. 'Madrid and…um… A few other places.'

An idea flashed into his head. One that, as he turned it over a few times and examined it more closely for potential flaws, seemed remarkably brilliant and foolproof.

'Come with me to Madrid for a few days.'

She blinked at him. 'What?'

'I have some meetings to attend in our office there.' Meetings that were currently scheduled for next week, but he would have Lucia bring them forward. 'I have an apartment in a separate building from the offices—near the Museo de Prado.'

She put her fork down. 'You'll be working during the day?'

'Of course. And you'll be busy sightseeing. I'll put a dedicated car and driver at your disposal. And then the evenings and the nights…' he pushed his chair back, reached for her hand and pulled her into his lap '…will be ours.'

It was perfect. Jordan wanted to see Madrid, and he wanted more of Jordan. One night together was not going to be enough. And taking her out of Barcelona was ideal. It eliminated any risk of her encountering his brother or anyone else from the family.

She bit her lip. 'I don't know…'

He rose with her in his arms and saw that adorable scowl forming on her features. But he also saw her pupils widen, heard her breathing grow shallow. She wanted him again already, and given how she'd come apart in his arms earlier he didn't imagine one night would be enough for her either.

'Hey!' She wriggled her luscious body against his. 'What are you doing? I'm not finished eating.'

His body hardening rapidly with need, he headed for the bedroom. 'It seems you may need some persuading.'

She opened her mouth and closed it again.

He lifted an eyebrow. 'Objections?'

Her scowl receded. 'No. But I warn you now—' she looped her arms around his neck '—I may need an *awful* lot of convincing.'

CHAPTER NINE

'OH, MY GOODNESS…' Jordan stepped off the bottom tread of the long staircase that had brought them deep underground and looked around her. 'This is amazing.'

She glanced up at Xavier and his easy smile, combined with the warm press of his palm against the small of her back, had a dangerous effect on her equilibrium.

He turned her towards an approaching maître d'. 'Four hundred years ago this was a network of winery cellars run by monks,' he said. 'Now it's one of Madrid's finest restaurants.'

The windowless space might have felt stuffy and oppressive, but it had been so beautifully restored that instead it felt welcoming and intimate.

Following the maître d', they walked beneath centuries-old arches of brick and stone, through an enchanting labyrinth of narrow passageways that linked a series of dining alcoves and galleries of varying shapes and sizes.

Isolated from the noisy, bustling city above, and with soft music piped through invisible speakers and subtle, atmospheric lighting enhancing the sense of tranquillity and seclusion, it was the perfect place for a couple to enjoy a romantic night out.

Ignoring the pang behind her ribs that warned her against yearning for things she shouldn't, Jordan smiled and thanked the man who'd shown them to their table, set in its own alcove, and held out her chair.

This was *not* a romantic date. She and Xavier were simply marking their third and final night in Madrid by doing something different. Something other than spending the whole evening at the apartment and ordering in.

Not that she'd minded that, of course. She'd packed her days with sightseeing, and by the time the evenings had rolled around all she'd wanted to do was see Xavier. She hadn't cared what they did, so long as they were together. But when he'd suggested they dine at a restaurant tonight she'd thrilled to the idea of going out with him.

A waiter brought the wine Xavier had ordered, noted their food selections and disappeared.

'What did you do today, *querida*?'

She smiled. When he'd asked that question last night, and the night before that, she'd been naked and sated, lying in his arms with her head resting on his chest. The first time she'd assumed he was just being polite, making conversation because that was what men thought women wanted. She'd expected him to listen with only half an ear, but his murmured comments and further questions had proved he was listening attentively and she'd realised his interest was genuine.

She sat forward and gave him a brief rundown of her day's sightseeing, which included, among other things, a visit to an impressive art museum housed in a neo-classical palace, a walk to one of the city's oldest squares, and a wander around the boat lake in Madrid's beautiful Retiro Park.

He frowned. 'You could have saved your feet a lot of walking if you'd accepted my offer of a driver.'

She shook her head. 'I told you. I like walking. And you see so much more than you do from the window of a car.'

He sipped his wine. He looked ultra-gorgeous tonight, his jaw dark with five o'clock shadow and his bronzed skin set off by a black open-collared shirt. 'Did you reach your friend?'

She pulled her gaze off the triangle of dusky skin at the base of his throat. 'Yes.'

'And everything is fine?'

She hesitated. 'Yes. A friend of hers is housesitting for me in Melbourne. She wanted to let me know that a local real estate agent had been in touch to say he has an interested buyer.'

She'd woken this morning to a text message from Ellie.

We need to talk!

Xavier, on his way out to the office, had seen her frown, asked her what was wrong, then told her to use the apartment's landline to call Australia.

Jordan wasn't lying about the estate agent. But that hadn't been Ellie's main bit of news. A nursing position was coming available in the emergency department at the Sydney hospital where Jordan had worked and where Ellie still did. Jordan had been well regarded during her time there, and the nurse manager had asked Ellie about Jordan's availability.

She would still have to go through the formal application channels, which meant cutting her trip short by a week and flying to Sydney for an interview, but the odds of her landing the position were good.

Ellie had almost squealed with excitement. And it *was* incredible news. To go home and practically walk back into her old job would be a solid first step towards getting her life back on track.

So why didn't she feel more excited? And why was she reluctant to tell Xavier about it?

Perhaps she simply wasn't ready for 'real life' to intrude just yet. For this fairytale bubble she felt as if she were floating in to burst.

'You own a house?'

'I inherited it. It's the home my father and Camila owned.'

'And you wish to sell it?'

A weight dragged at her chest for a moment. She'd had some happy times in that house, but the people she'd shared those times with were both gone.

'I haven't made up my mind, but I suspect that's what I'll end up doing. Even if I stay in Melbourne the house is too big for me. It was too big for Dad and Camila, really, but it's right by the ocean and Camila adored the sea—' She caught herself. 'Sorry,' she muttered, dropping her gaze to her wine glass. 'I know you're not interested—'

'Don't.' Xavier reached across the table and covered her hand with his. His mouth firmed, but his voice was soft. 'If anyone should apologise it is me.'

Her skin tingled under the warm pressure of his fingers. Heart beating a little faster, she looked up. 'What for?'

His thumb stroked over her knuckles. 'For what I said in the car on Sunday. It was disrespectful. It is not my place to judge Camila or to make assumptions about the situation she found herself in. The fact is she made a choice thirty-five years ago that was ultimately for my benefit, and for that I am grateful to her.'

Jordan's throat stung, and for a moment she had to look away. She swallowed, then let her gaze connect again with his. 'Thank you. That means a lot to me—and it would have meant a lot to Camila.'

He caressed her knuckles once more and then withdrew his hand. As he did so Jordan noticed a man watching them from a table in another alcove, just visible beyond Xavier's left shoulder. She didn't recognise him, or his beautiful female companion, but he held her gaze for a moment before looking away.

Xavier brought her attention back to him. 'When did you lose your father?'

'Four years ago,' she said quietly. 'It was a stroke. Sudden and unexpected.'

'I'm sorry.'

She smiled sadly. 'Me, too. He was a wonderful man. Very gentle and kind.'

He was silent for a moment. 'And your mother?'

She shook her head. 'She left when I was six. I don't have a relationship with her.'

She rarely spoke of her mother. It had been twenty years since Jacqueline Walsh had left the house to go to her precious job and not bothered coming home to her husband and daughter. Jordan had buried that hurt a long time ago, somewhere very deep.

'Dad met Camila when I was ten and they married a year later. From then on she was who I thought of as my mom.' She pushed a smile onto her face. 'They were lovely together. Truly happy. The perfect couple.' Emotion knotted her throat again, and she quickly moved on. 'Speaking of happy couples—did you know that Rosa and Alfonso are about to have their thirtieth wedding anniversary?'

'I did.'

Jordan pulled her chin back and blinked. 'Really?'

Her patent disbelief earned her a look of wounded affront.

'You think I'm a cold, heartless boss who knows nothing about his employees?'

When she hesitated a second too long his eyes narrowed and his voice turned low and silky.

'I see I shall have to disabuse you of some of your erroneous notions later tonight.'

Laughter rose in her throat then, and her pulse skipped in her veins. This lighter, teasing side of Xavier never failed to surprise and delight her.

The fact that neither of them had yet broached the question of what would happen when they returned to Barcelona tomorrow was something she chose not to think about just now.

'So naturally you've given them both some time off so they can celebrate?' she challenged.

'*Sí*. Along with first-class air tickets to Berlin to see their daughter and son-in-law.'

Suddenly her insides went a little mushy. 'Rosa didn't mention you were doing that.'

'She doesn't know. Alfonso is surprising her. He came to me a few months ago, without Rosa's knowledge, to discuss the two of them having some time off. They haven't seen their daughter in a long time and he wanted to take Rosa to Germany for their anniversary. I agreed to the time off on the proviso that he allow me to pay their airfares.'

Ridiculously, her eyes welled. 'Oh, Xavier. That… that's such a lovely thing to do.'

He shrugged. 'They've given me ten years of loyal service. It is something small I can do to show my appreciation.'

Only a billionaire would dismiss such a gesture as 'small'. She swallowed down the silly lump in her throat. It was difficult to reconcile the man in front of her—a man who clearly had a generous heart buried inside that impressive chest of his—with the one who'd expressed such cold, clinical views about love and marriage.

What could possibly have happened to him to make him so cynical?

Quelling her curiosity, she asked, 'When are they going?'

'Tomorrow. For ten days.'

'Ten days without Rosa's cooking? That's a lot of takeout,' she teased.

He twisted the stem of his wine glass between his thumb and forefinger. 'Stay,' he said suddenly, fixing his gaze on hers.

Her heart stalled for a moment, then took off at a frantic pace.

'While Rosa and Alfonso are away?'

'Sí.'

She willed her pulse-rate to calm. For a split second she'd thought—

'I'll take you to Mallorca over the weekend,' he said. 'And London the following weekend.'

Her heart sank a tiny bit. She thought of the private jet they'd flown in, of his luxury homes in Barcelona and Madrid, then tried to imagine the sort of opulent place they would stay in Mallorca or London. Was this the kind of incentive he thought would keep her in his bed for another week? The promise of free luxury travel and swanky accommodation?

He didn't know her at all. If he did he'd know she would settle for the promise of something far simpler and less expensive—like a whole uninterrupted day with him. A whole twenty-four hours with no work, no phone calls, no emails… Nothing but him and her, talking, teasing, getting to know one another…making love.

She looked down, twirling her glass between her hands. Maybe the high life was what wealthy men expected their mistresses to demand.

Mistresses.

Ugh. Was that what this fling, or affair, or whatever you called it, made her? A rich man's mistress?

'I'm not sure,' she said, lifting her gaze and accidentally catching the eye of the man she'd noticed earlier. She quickly looked away and focused on Xavier. 'Let me think about it.'

His eyes held hers again, and suddenly the air shimmered with a potent mix of heat and sensuality. 'Do I need to remind you how persuasive I can be, *amante*?'

Desire tugged in her belly, so intense it almost took her breath away, and she wondered if he was right about a passion like theirs having an expiry date. If he was, would she be foolish to walk away from it prematurely? To deny herself the enjoyment of something she might never experience again?

The waiter reappeared then, with their starters, and they ate and moved on to an easier, less sexually charged conversation.

She was fascinated by the multiple facets of his family's business—or perhaps it was his obvious commitment and passion for his work that captivated her as he patiently answered her questions.

And saddened her.

How would his future wife and children ever compete for his attention when his work consumed him so completely?

Her heart ached at the thought of his children—Camila's grandchildren—feeling the way her mother had made her feel.

Unloved. Unimportant. *Unwanted.*

And yet… Xavier had made it clear he wanted a family, hadn't he? Moreover, when she'd questioned whether he would love his children he'd reacted almost angrily. Which had to mean…what? That he believed in parental love but not in love between a man and a woman?

Why not the latter? He was capable of tenderness. Affection. She experienced that side of him every time he held her in the aftermath of their lovemaking. Every time his strong arms cocooned her and held her to his side, or her back snuggled against his front. He made her feel protected and cherished. Made her long for something deeper, stronger, more permanent than just sexual gratification.

Was that how his future wife was destined to feel? Would she forever yearn for something her husband wasn't willing to give? Or would her patience be rewarded? Because surely it wasn't a leap too far to think that tenderness and affection could eventually turn into love…

Jordan reached for her wine, her hand a little unsteady as she took a sip. She was letting her thoughts drift along a dangerous path. Maybe even subconsciously casting herself in the role of his future wife.

Which was crazy. Xavier desired her—she didn't doubt that—but she would never fit the mould of perfect corporate wife.

Annoyed with herself, she put down her glass, picked up the dessert menu and concentrated on reading it. Everything looked divine, but she'd eaten so much already.

'The cheesecake sounds good,' she mused. 'But I'm not sure I have the room.'

'We could share one,' Xavier suggested.

And in the end they did—and Jordan told herself that it wasn't the *slightest* bit romantic.

They finished off with *digestifs* of brandy—and that was when the male diner whose eye she'd been studiously avoiding stood up and approached their table. She opened her mouth to warn Xavier but she was too late. The man was already beside him, clapping a hand over his shoulder.

'Buenas noches, querido primo.'

Xavier's entire body tensed, and before he even looked up and acknowledged the other man the atmosphere grew frigid.

Jaw locked tight, he sat back in an abrupt way that forced the man's hand off his shoulder. 'Diego.'

Gone were the relaxed lines of his face and the smoky warmth in his silver-grey eyes. His expression was fixed and unreadable. The men exchanged a few sentences in Spanish, and Jordan didn't need to understand the language to know these two weren't friends. Their tones weren't aggressive, but Xavier's words were clipped, his body language closed-off, and although the other man smiled there was an antagonistic quality to his manner.

More than once his gaze strayed to her, but Xavier

made no effort to introduce her and she grew increasingly uncomfortable.

Then, abruptly, the man turned to her and stuck out his hand. *'Hola, soy Diego de la Vega. Mucho gusto.'*

Jordan froze. De la Vega? These two were *family*?

Not wanting to appear rude, she put her hand in his and said simply, 'Jordan Walsh.'

Instantly she regretted offering her hand. The way he gripped her fingers and sent his gaze travelling down her body, as if he didn't already have a beautiful woman waiting back at his table, made her skin crawl.

'Ah, you are English?'

She reclaimed her hand. 'Australian,' she said automatically, then wished she hadn't when she flicked her gaze to Xavier and saw his face darken.

He stood so quickly his chair scraped on the stone floor, and the physical dissimilarity between the two men was immediately apparent. Diego de la Vega was good-looking, but he didn't have Xavier's height or the same powerful build, and he didn't possess one iota of the raw masculinity and charisma Xavier exuded.

He looked at her. 'Let's go,' he said evenly, and she didn't need further prompting.

Whoever he was, Diego de la Vega made her uneasy; she was more than happy to leave.

Fortunately Xavier had already paid the bill. He said a curt *'Buenas noches'* to his relative, and then they made a quick exit—though not before Jordan had fielded a look from Diego that not only glinted with ill-concealed curiosity but also, she thought, a hint of malevolence.

Suppressing a shudder, she emerged onto the street

and turned to Xavier. His jaw was still tight, his mouth compressed. 'Who *was* that?'

'My cousin.'

Hand on her elbow, he guided her into the back of the chauffeured vehicle that waited at the kerb for them. He joined her from the other side and then stayed frustratingly silent.

After two minutes of his brooding, she could no longer hold her tongue. 'Why is there so much animosity between you two?'

He continued to look out of his window. 'We don't get along.'

She stared at his profile, so strong and proud. So achingly handsome. 'I could see that,' she said patiently. 'I'm asking you why.'

He paused for so long she thought he wasn't going to answer. 'We fell out over a woman.'

Jordan was silent as she absorbed that. So he had once felt strongly enough about a woman to feel territorial over her?

'Recently?' she asked, conscious of a hot, unaccountable twinge of jealousy.

'Ten years ago.'

Foolishly, she felt relieved. 'Is that why you didn't introduce me?'

He turned his head to look at her, and she cringed inwardly, knowing that he must have heard the hint of hurt in her voice.

The truth was she *did* feel hurt. Regardless of this spat the two men had had a decade ago, Diego was Xavier's family—and yet he hadn't thought her important enough to introduce. Perhaps he'd thought he was protecting her—and admittedly Diego *had* unnerved her—but at the same time Xavier had made her feel small. Insignificant.

'He's not a nice man, *querida*.'

His voice was gentler now, but Jordan sensed he was holding something back. Something more serious than a fight over a woman.

'What else?'

He frowned. 'What do you mean?'

'There's something else,' she pressed, running with her instincts. 'Besides the woman. Some other reason you and Diego don't get along.'

He looked out of his window again, silent for another long moment. *'Sí,'* he said at last. 'But it's… complicated.'

'You don't think I can understand "complicated"?'

'I don't think it's anything you really want to hear about.'

'If I wasn't interested,' she said gently, 'I wouldn't have asked.'

He pulled in a breath and released it slowly. Then he turned back to her. 'There are certain members of the extended de la Vega family—including Diego and his father, Hector, who is my father's first cousin—who have never accepted me as one of them.'

It was Jordan's turn to frown. 'One of "them"?'

'A de la Vega.'

She was silent for a moment, trying to make sense of what he was telling her. She thought she understood, and yet it seemed ludicrous. Unbelievable.

'Because you're adopted?'

'Sí.' His voice was tight. 'Because my veins do not run with true blue de la Vega blood.'

She felt a spurt of outrage. 'But…that's ridiculous!'

His smile was grim. 'That is the way of it.'

'So they…what? Ignore you at family gatherings? Leave you off the invitation list?'

He gave a humourless laugh. 'If only it were that simple.'

'What, then?'

He shook his head. 'You don't want to know about these things, *querida*.'

'I do,' she insisted, turning sideways in her seat— as much as her seatbelt would allow—to see him better. 'Tell me.'

He blew out another breath. 'For more than sixty years the position of CEO of the Vega Corporation has been handed down from father to son. My grandfather and Diego's grandfather were brothers. They both wanted the position. But my grandfather, as the eldest, was given the role. The rivalry between the brothers continued to the next generation, to their sons—'

'Your father and Diego's father?'

'*Sí*. My grandfather handed the position to my father, Vittorio, and he, in turn, handed the reins to me five years ago.'

'And Diego's father didn't like that?' she surmised.

'Hector's stance has always been that I have no birth right to any part of the family business. As a board member he officially objected when the CEO role was offered to me, but he couldn't garner enough support from the rest of the board to veto my appointment.'

She shook her head, appalled. 'That's snobbery and prejudice.'

'It's more than that. Hector is power-hungry. He wants me out and Diego in.'

'Diego as CEO?' After one brief encounter she

barely knew the man, but her gut told her his leadership qualities would pale next to Xavier's. 'But what about your adoptive brother?'

'Ramon has never had any interest in the top job.' Another mirthless smile curved Xavier's lips. 'He says he's allergic to board meetings.'

'And your father?'

Surely Vittorio de la Vega didn't idly stand by while his adopted son was vilified by his own family.

'He stood down as Chairman last year after a health scare—problems with his heart. He remains on the board but he's taken a step back from the politicking. I prefer it that way. I don't want him stressed. He's given his pound of flesh to the business over the years—and he trusts that I can handle whatever Hector throws at me.'

Jordan heard both concern and respect in Xavier's voice. 'You care for him very much?'

'Of course.' He spoke without hesitation. 'For both of my parents. They're good people. The attitude of certain family members towards me has been...difficult for them. Upsetting.'

'And for you?' she queried gently.

He shrugged. 'It has simply made me work harder—to prove I can be better than the likes of Diego and Hector.'

Jordan felt her heart squeeze. Looking at him now, armed with this new knowledge, she saw so much more than a proud, driven, ambitious workaholic. She saw a man who'd had to work hard to prove himself over and over again. Who'd had to fight for acceptance and no doubt watch his back every step of the way.

It was no wonder he came across as arrogant and formidable at times. A man who had enemies constantly attempting to undermine him couldn't afford to show weakness.

Her chest burned with outrage. 'Were they cruel to you when you were a child?'

Another dismissive shrug. 'Diego and a few other cousins on his side of the family resorted to taunts and name-calling when the adults were out of earshot. It was nothing I couldn't handle.'

'What sort of names?'

'Nothing suitable for your delicate ears.'

She scowled. 'I wish I'd known all this when I met Diego at the restaurant. I would have punched that slimeball in the nose!'

Xavier looked at her, shocked, and then he threw his head back and laughed, the sound deliciously deep and full-bodied as it reverberated around the car's interior.

His voice was rich with amusement when he spoke. 'That is very sweet, *querida*, but I'm willing to bet you've never hit anyone in your life.'

'There's a first time for everything,' she muttered, and then sucked in her breath to say more.

But he moved suddenly, and before she could guess what he intended he'd removed her seatbelt and dragged her onto his lap.

'Enough talking,' he growled. 'I can think of better things to do with my mouth.'

Shock—and a surge of anticipation—made her voice breathy. 'What happened to being safety-conscious?'

His silver eyes glittered. 'You're safe in my arms, *amante*.'

She wasn't so sure about that, given the look of carnal intent on his face.

Then he stroked his hand over her breast and pressed

an open-mouthed kiss to the base of her throat, and suddenly the last thing on Jordan's mind was being careful—or safe...

At six-forty-five a.m. on Friday they boarded his jet on the tarmac in Madrid for their return to Barcelona.

Jordan hadn't complained about their early rising, but she had looked deliciously flushed and dishevelled as she'd raced around the apartment gathering up her things before the car arrived.

Her last-minute rush to pack had been his fault. He'd joined her in the shower, pressed her back against the tiles and done things to her under the steaming water that had consequently made them both run late—but she hadn't complained about that either.

In the final minutes before they'd left the apartment she'd flown back into the bedroom, looking for something, and Xav had spied her journal on a side table in the living room. It had lain open at a page on which she'd written her list of things to see and do in Spain, and although he hadn't intended to look one item had caught his eye before he'd closed the journal and called out to her that he'd found it.

The flight crew readied the aircraft for take-off and for the next hour Jordan dozed. Curled up on the seat next to him, head resting on his shoulder, she teased his senses with her subtle floral scent and soft, feminine warmth.

Time and again he found his gaze resting on her instead of on the document he'd opened on his tablet. Even in sleep she glowed with that irrepressible vitality that belied the pain she'd suffered. She wasn't yet thirty, yet already she'd lost two parents—three if you included her biological mother.

He felt a touch of anger when he thought of Jordan being abandoned by her mother. She'd skimmed over the fact as if it barely mattered to her, but no one, especially a child, could weather that sort of rejection without sustaining a few psychological scars.

Had his own biological mother played an instrumental role in healing Jordan's wounds?

He tucked a stray curl behind her ear and for the first time felt a deep sadness in his chest at the thought that he would never meet his birth mother. Jordan had loved and respected her stepmother; that fact alone told him Camila Walsh had been a good woman.

His mind turned to the letter she'd written to him— the letter he'd not yet read—and it struck him then, with a force that made the breath jam in his throat, what a gift it was. A gift he held in his possession only because Jordan had come halfway around the world to deliver it to him.

On impulse he pressed a kiss to the top of her head and she stirred, tipping up her chin and blinking sleepily at him.

'Are we there?'

Her lips were soft and pink, and he studied the plump contours with a mix of lust and tenderness. Last night, after leaving the restaurant, he'd told her things he'd never revealed to another woman, opening up in a way he ordinarily would have found discomfiting. Instead it had deepened the sense of intimacy between them, so that later, when he had taken her to bed, when he'd joined his body with hers in the most intimate way possible, their physical connection had felt much more unique and powerful.

Had Jordan felt it, too? Was that why she'd finally agreed to stay for another week?

He brushed his fingers over the satin slope of her cheek and for a moment felt intensely envious of the man who would one day fulfil her romantic dream of love and happily-ever-after. He couldn't be that man—he would never lay himself bare to that kind of risk and expectation—but for now she was his, and he would give and take as much pleasure as their time together allowed.

He stroked the pad of his thumb over her bottom lip and smiled. 'Not yet, *querida*,' he murmured. 'Go back to sleep.'

At a little after two-thirty Xav stood at the window of his office, staring out across the city, his mind adrift until the sound of Ramon's dry, half-amused voice dragged him out of his head.

'Daydreaming, *hermano*?'

He turned, shot a deliberate look at his watch and raised an eyebrow. 'Did you forget to set your alarm?' He eyed his brother as he sauntered in and sat down in front of his desk. 'I came to the office from Madrid and managed to get here five hours earlier than you.'

Ramon shrugged, unconcerned. 'Katie had a bad night, which means Emily had a bad night. I stayed at the villa this morning to look after Katie so Em could rest.'

That didn't sound like his sister-in-law. Emily might look delicate, but he knew she was a strong, capable woman. Not the type to be fazed by a sleepless night. 'She's unwell?'

'She's fine, but she had a virus a couple of weeks ago. She tires easily.'

He sat down behind his desk. 'Mamá couldn't have helped?'

'She offered, but she had some errands to run, and then one of her luncheons in the city, so I told her to go.' He stretched out his legs. 'How was Madrid?'

'Fine. Mostly meetings. No dramas.'

If he didn't count running into their cousin Diego. Unease ran through him like a trickle of icy water, but he shook off the sense of foreboding. Diego had witnessed nothing last night that he could wield as a weapon. He'd seen his cousin dining out with a beautiful woman—that was all. It was unfortunate that Jordan had revealed her full name, but Diego would have to dig deep and connect a lot of obscure dots before he unearthed anything significant.

Xav leaned back in his chair and took a breath. 'I can't make it tomorrow,' he said, and saw surprise flash across his brother's face.

'Why not?'

'I have another commitment.'

One with red hair, soft curves and a ripe mouth he seemed to have developed a permanent craving for.

Ramon frowned. 'You haven't seen Emily or Katie yet. Em will be disappointed. We're returning to London on Sunday.'

'I'm sorry.'

Ruthlessly he quashed the flare of guilt. His time with Jordan was limited, whereas his family would always be relatively close and accessible. His parents' home was a thirty-minute drive from his. Ramon and his family, in London, were only two hours away by plane. He could see any of them any time—just not this weekend.

Ramon held his palms up. 'Fine. I assume you've told Mamá?'

'I'll call her.'

Although it wasn't a conversation he looked forward to. Very rarely did he disappoint his mother. For years that had been Ramon's speciality, and Xav had lost count of the times he'd taken his brother to task for his self-ish behaviour.

Things were different now, of course. Ramon was different. He'd settled down, returned to the family fold.

Another trickle of unease went down Xav's spine. Now *he* was the one about to upset their mother. Was that what his lust for Jordan had reduced him to? Was she his drug of choice and he little better than a junkie who would do anything—even lie to and disappoint his family—to guarantee his next fix?

'You can tell her in person.'

He looked at his brother. 'Excuse me?'

'Mamá. She's coming here after lunch.' Ramon glanced at his watch and frowned. 'If you haven't seen her, then she's late. She said she'd be here around two. Unless…'

A sudden ripple of tension went through Xav's shoulders. 'Unless what?'

Ramon grimaced. 'She might have gone to the apartment first. I let slip about the renovation, and you know how she likes to put her two cents in when it comes to decorating. Sorry, *hermano*. She's probably up there right now changing the entire colour scheme.'

'*She* is right here, *mis queridos hijos*, so be careful what you say.'

Both men straightened in their chairs and swung their gazes towards the doorway.

Elena de la Vega smiled at her sons. Then she walked into the office and placed an elegant hand on Ramon's shoulder.

'*Querido*, would you give me a moment alone with your brother, please?' She waited for the door to close behind him, then sat in the chair he'd vacated, fixed her caramel-brown eyes on her eldest son and said, 'I've just had an interesting conversation with the very beautiful and utterly charming young woman in your apartment.'

CHAPTER TEN

JORDAN PACED THE full length of the living area at least a dozen times before she paused, took a deep breath and told herself to calm down.

But she couldn't.

How could she be calm when she knew Xavier was going to be furious? *Livid.*

If only she'd stayed out a bit longer. Explored a few more of the quaint streets in the city's medieval Gothic Quarter. But three days of full-on sightseeing in Madrid and four nights of vigorous lovemaking had finally taken their toll. The idea of whiling away the afternoon with a book, stretched out on one of the loungers by the apartment's pool, had been too tempting to resist.

And then Xavier's mother had walked into the apartment.

His *mother.*

Her stomach tied in knots, she began to pace again, her bare feet taking her on another circuit of the living area and then out onto the sun-warmed terrace. But the fresh air didn't help; her mind continued to spin in ever-decreasing circles, tighter and tighter, until her thoughts narrowed down to a single, soul-crushing certainty.

He would end it now.

He would be so angry about what she'd told his mother he'd change his mind about her staying and ask her to leave.

And this time his rejection wouldn't just sting, like it had the night he'd spurned her by the pool. It would burn. Painfully. Horribly.

Because she cared now. More than she had before.

How could she not? They'd been intimate together. They'd shared things. Oh, she wasn't fooling herself with romantic delusions. She understood this was an affair, not a proper relationship. But she'd have to be carved from stone to feel absolutely nothing.

And she knew him better now. He was proud and honourable and generous and hardworking. She didn't only desire him, she liked him. Respected him.

Oh, come on. It's more than that.

Desperately she shut out the voice in her head. Feelings of love—true love—took time to develop. You couldn't fall head over heels for someone in less than two weeks…

With a groan of despair—because she feared that was precisely what she'd done—she stopped again and covered her face with her hands.

For a moment—just a moment—she thought about how easy it would be to flee. Not to have to face Xavier. To avoid his anger, the inevitable rejection—

'Jordan?'

She froze. *No.* She wasn't ready for him. Not yet. She needed more time. More time to shore up her emotional defences. More time to slip into whatever kind of cool demeanour mistresses adopted when they were about to be unceremoniously dumped.

'What are you doing?'

Did he sound angry? She couldn't tell.

She pulled in a deep breath, dropped her hands and faced him. He moved towards her, as darkly handsome as ever in his tailored suit, his short hair glossy black in the sunlight. His expression was serious but not, she registered with a rush of surprised relief, angry.

Perhaps it was that which gave her the courage to answer candidly. 'I don't know… Panicking, I think.'

She huffed out a small, self-deprecating laugh, but Xavier's expression remained serious.

'Why?'

She eyed him warily. 'Has your mother spoken with you?'

He came closer. *'Sí.'*

Her shoulders slumped under the weight of guilt. 'I'm so sorry,' she said in a rush. 'I got such a shock when she walked in—I'm sure she did, too. And then she introduced herself and I realised she was your mother and… She was so lovely… I was just—I couldn't lie to her about who I was. It felt wrong—'

She broke off and looked at him, feeling utterly wretched, conscious she was babbling. She felt as discomposed as she had the day he'd summoned her to his study at the villa. Why did he have this effect on her? No one else had ever done this to her. Turned her into a flustered, scatterbrained wreck.

She tipped her head back to look at him, said hesitantly, 'Aren't you angry?'

He lifted his hands and curled them over her shoulders, his thumbs brushing the sides of her neck. 'That you respected my mother by not lying to her?' He shook his head. 'No, *querida*. I'm not angry.'

Another surge of relief, this one even more power-

ful, made her legs feel weak. Or maybe that was simply the impact of Xavier standing so close. She'd lost
count of how many times they'd made love, yet still her
body ached for his touch so intensely it frightened her.

'I still feel awful,' she confessed, letting her hands
slide up between them, flattening her palms on his
chest. She couldn't stand this close and not touch him.
'Talking with your parents about Camila was something you were entitled to do in your own time, whenever it felt right. Now, because of me, it's been forced
on you...' She bit her lip. 'Was she upset?'

The sides of his thumbs idly stroked up and down her
neck, sending tiny shivers of sensation across her skin.

'Only a little. My mother has a very understanding nature.'

'Do you think she guessed that we're...?' She felt
her face flame. 'You know...'

He gave a glimmer of a smile. 'Having a relationship?'

Her heart missed a beat. *Relationship?* Was that how
he thought of their affair? She nodded, telling herself
not to read anything into it.

It's just a word.

'She didn't ask me outright,' he said. 'But I suspect
she's guessed.'

Jordan let out a little groan of embarrassment, her
gaze darting down to her T-shirt and shorts. Elena de
la Vega had been pleasant and friendly, but what must
she have been secretly thinking? That her son's standards had dropped considerably from the sophisticated
women he usually saw, no doubt.

Xavier, as though he'd read her mind, tilted her chin
up and said, 'She thought you were very charming. And
very beautiful.'

Her eyes widened. 'She did?'

'*Sí.*' He paused, his gaze moving thoughtfully over her face for a long moment. 'In fact you've made such an impression she's asked me to invite you to a luncheon at my parents' house tomorrow.'

She blinked. 'Really? Gosh, I...' Her heart beat a little faster. *Lunch with his parents?* 'How do you feel about that?' she asked carefully.

'I think if I fail to persuade you to accept my mother will be extremely disappointed and I may never hear the end of it.'

An evasive answer, revealing nothing of his true thoughts.

Jordan pressed her lips together, silencing the urge to push, to dig for some declaration of feeling that would probably never exist outside her fantasies.

Anyhow, perhaps it didn't matter what Xavier thought or felt. The invitation was from Elena de la Vega, not her son. Jordan had liked her immensely—had felt a bond of sorts as soon as they'd started talking about Camila.

Elena's eyes had clouded with sadness and compassion on learning of Camila's passing, and then with tears when Jordan had explained that she'd met Xavier because she'd brought a letter to him that her stepmom had written.

She'd hoped Elena might assume that she was simply staying as a house guest at the apartment, but if the older woman had already guessed something more was going on... Well, there wasn't anything to hide, then, was there?

Her mind made up, she smiled. 'It's kind of your

mother to invite me, and I wouldn't want to disappoint her—or offend her. So…yes. I accept.'

'Good,' he said, although she couldn't tell whether he truly meant it.

He dropped a swift, perfunctory kiss on her mouth that was barely satisfying, then took his hands off her shoulders. Immediately her body craved their weight and warmth again. She let her own hands fall from his chest before the desire to grab his shirt and pull him back for a proper kiss overpowered her.

He glanced at his watch. 'I won't be later than six. We'll stay at the villa tonight, *sì*?'

She nodded, pasting on a bright smile that slid off her mouth as soon as he was gone.

Xavier mightn't have been angry, but he hadn't looked particularly happy, either.

Jordan dressed for lunch in a simple sleeveless pale lemon sundress she'd bought on impulse from a boutique sale in Madrid, and paired it with open-toed shoes. She carefully applied a bit of make-up, attached plain gold hoops to her ears, and was attempting to scrape her hair into some kind of sophisticated up-do when Xavier came up behind her, gently pulled her wrists down and removed the few pins she'd already inserted.

'I prefer it down,' he said, holding her gaze in the mirror until heat began to surge and eddy around them.

He was clean from the shower and wore nothing but a white towel loosely around his hips, and the mere sight of all that hard, masculine flesh sent tingles racing over her skin.

'Xavier…' she whispered, her tone a mix of plea and admonishment. 'We don't have time.'

He grinned, which made her pulse skip, then kissed her shoulder and moved away, leaving her to deal with suppressed desire on top of a belly full of nerves.

Nerves that had doubled in intensity ever since he'd mentioned that she would meet not only his parents at lunch, but his brother, Ramon, and his wife and their four-month-old baby daughter, who were visiting from London.

They drove to his parents' villa in the Aston Martin. It made a nice change from sitting in the back of chauffeured vehicles, and she sensed that Xavier enjoyed being behind the wheel.

His mood was lighter this morning, making her wonder if yesterday's quieter, more pensive mood had resulted from work issues rather than his mother's unexpected visit.

Whatever had set him brooding, it hadn't affected his sex drive, though. Last night's lovemaking had been intense and mind-blowing, his demands on her body exquisitely relentless. When she'd clung to him weakly and whimpered that she couldn't possibly climax again he had seemed to take it as a personal challenge, and had set about driving her to yet another shattering peak with ruthless, breathtaking mastery.

They'd even made love in the pool, where the cool, satiny feel of the water against hot, naked skin had intensified every sensation.

Jordan felt deeply grateful and relieved that Rosa and Alfonso were in Berlin, for they surely would have heard her wild screams of release from the staff cottage.

She took a deep breath now, as Xavier braked to a stop in front of Elena and Vittorio de la Vega's beautiful traditional white villa.

Perhaps sensing she was nervous, he lifted her hand and kissed her knuckles. 'You look beautiful,' he murmured, and her heart swelled with an emotion she tried very hard to suppress.

And then, before they'd even emerged from the car, Elena was there, the warmth of her smile and her effusive greeting like an instant balm to Jordan's nerves. She watched Xavier put an arm around his mother and kiss her cheek and it touched her deeply—maybe even made her feel a little bit hopeful—to see the obvious love and respect between mother and son.

Whatever beliefs Xavier held about himself, he *was* capable of love.

They walked with Elena through the villa, and just before they stepped out onto the shaded terrace where the others were gathered Xavier linked his hand with hers, entwining their fingers, tugging her to his side.

The gesture felt both intimate and proprietorial and, knowing it would send a message to his family about their relationship, she sent him a quizzical look. But his expression was enigmatic, giving her no steer on exactly what message he wanted to send, so she simply went with it, telling herself to enjoy it without overanalysing.

And enjoy herself she did. So much so that after three pleasurable hours it felt strangely wrenching to say goodbye to these people she'd only just met and barely knew.

Ramon's wife, Emily, hugged her and slipped her a business card with her personal mobile number jotted on the back. 'Call me if you make it to London. I'd love to catch up. And if you're in the market for babysitting, definitely call me.' She grinned. 'I've never seen Katie sit so happily in a stranger's lap before. She adores you!'

On the drive home she felt an oddly melancholy mood slip over her, and she sat quietly in the front passenger seat, content to watch the scenery until Xavier's voice gently penetrated her thoughts.

'Querida?'

She turned her head to look at him. 'Sorry? What was that?'

'Is everything all right?'

She offered up a smile. 'Yes, of course.'

There was a pause. 'You didn't enjoy yourself this afternoon?'

'I had a wonderful time,' she quickly assured him.

'But something has upset you?'

She shook her head. 'Nothing's upset me.' She really *had* had a lovely time. 'I just…'

He took his eyes off the road for a second to glance at her. 'What?'

She was silent for a long moment. She didn't know how to articulate what she was feeling. Not without sounding envious and self-pitying.

Finally she just said, 'You have an amazing family, Xavier. Don't ever take them for granted.'

Because one day they'll be gone, by choice or by fate, and you'll realise the people you love, and the ones who love you back, are rare gifts indeed.

Xav walked into the cool of the villa, set his keys down and drew Jordan into the circle of his arms.

She came to him without resistance, shaving the edge off his unease, quelling his concern at her strange turn of mood.

She'd been superb with his family, charming them all as he'd known she would. It was ironic that what he had at first viewed as a potential disaster yesterday had, in fact, been a catalyst for shifting his mind, and his intentions, in a direction he suspected they would have eventually gone anyway—just a little more slowly.

Of course he'd have preferred it if things had panned out in a different, more controlled way, but he appreciated how Jordan had handled her unexpected encounter with his mother. When he'd gone up to see her she'd been flustered, understandably, and given his own preoccupation with the unanticipated turn of events he perhaps had not consoled her as well as he could have.

But she seemed to have taken it all in her stride—another quality to add to her list of attributes.

He stroked her spine through the fabric of her pretty yellow dress. She looked good in anything she wore—and he rather liked those little denim shorts that showed off her legs—but it was nice to see her in something more feminine. It made him want to drape her in jewels—yellow sapphires and emeralds to match her eyes—and commission a dozen bespoke evening gowns that would showcase her luscious curves to perfection. She would, he knew, turn heads wherever they went.

'What do you want to do this afternoon, *querida*?'

She eyed him. 'Don't you have work to do?'

He did. Fifty-odd unopened emails, a bid for a multimillion-dollar construction project in Dubai awaiting sign-off, and the latest time-wasting communication from Reynaud's lawyers to read.

None of which, at this very second, mattered more than putting the smile back on Jordan's lips.

His mother's words, spoken today out of earshot of anyone else, came back to him.

'Go gently with her, Xavier. She is vulnerable. I like her and would not wish to see her hurt.'

He'd looked at his *mamá* and wondered if they were talking about the same woman. 'She's strong,' he'd countered. It was another of her qualities he admired.

'Yes,' Elena had agreed. 'But she is grieving—and strong people hurt, too. They are just better at making the world think they don't.' Then she'd reached up and patted his cheek. 'Rather like someone else I know.'

Of course his mother was not only perceptive and wise, she was right. Jordan was still grieving Camila's loss. Spending time with his family had reminded her of the loved ones she'd lost and precipitated this sudden bout of sadness.

He didn't like it. Didn't like the shadows in her eyes, the downturn of her lovely mouth.

'No work today,' he declared. 'Tell me what you want to do. Your wish is my command.'

She pressed a cool palm to his forehead and frowned. 'Are you feeling unwell, Senyor de la Vega? You don't seem yourself.'

He moulded her soft body to his, snugly enough for her to feel his arousal. 'Come to think of it...' he murmured. 'I do have an ache that may need some attention. What would you recommend?'

She pursed her lips, contemplating. 'I would suggest you go straight to bed.'

His lips quirked. 'Is that your professional opinion, Nurse Walsh?'

'It is,' she said solemnly.

'In that case—' he scooped her up and she laughed, and he thought it might be the sweetest sound he'd ever heard '—who am I to argue?'

CHAPTER ELEVEN

JORDAN FELT THE subtle shift in their relationship—and, yes, she was allowing herself to use that word loosely in her head—over the course of the weekend.

Some things were obvious. Xavier barely set foot inside his study, for instance, and there were several occasions when his phone was conspicuous by its absence—like when she'd made him take her on a hike to the highest point on the estate, a spot he admitted with some chagrin he'd never walked to before, and when they'd meandered down to his private beach for a naked moonlit dip in the ocean.

Other things were less obvious. Like the times she would look up from her book or a task and find his gaze resting on her, his expression pensive, enigmatic. Once or twice she felt as though she were being quietly assessed—though for what purpose she couldn't have said. The idea that he might be comparing her with former mistresses was, she discovered, an unpleasant thought that served only to send a hot streak of jealousy and insecurity through her.

'What are you thinking, *amante*?'

She lifted her head off the lounger. Sprawled in the one alongside her, he was a mouthwatering sight in nothing but a pair of black swimming trunks. He'd just swum fifty lengths of the pool and droplets of water glistened in his chest hair and snaked in rivulets over his taut, well-defined musculature.

She adjusted her sunglasses and tried not to ogle him. 'I'm not thinking about anything. I'm reading my book.'

'You've stared at the same page for the last ten minutes.'

She dropped the book into her lap. 'Men are not supposed to be that observant,' she grumbled, then smiled when he chuckled. She couldn't resist him in this mood.

'So what's on your mind?' he pressed.

Jordan put her book aside, pulled her knees up to her chest. 'Honestly?'

He looked at her, silent for a moment, as though sensing the tone of their conversation was about to change.

'Sí,' he invited. 'Honestly.'

She pushed her sunglasses onto her head, even though it would have been easier to hide behind them. But she couldn't always protect herself, could she? Lord knew she'd tried, ever since she was a child—making herself indispensable, ensuring she was needed, even choosing a profession that made her feel useful. Valued. But still she had lost the people she loved the most… her dad, Camila.

A week ago Xavier had accused her of running away, and he'd been right. Running away was easier than facing rejection. Hadn't she even tried to leave his bed after the first time they'd made love? Fearing that if she didn't he would throw her out of it? He hadn't. Just as he hadn't demanded she leave on Friday, after his mother had visited, even though—to her shame—one of her first thoughts had been to flee.

And now… Now she wanted to be brave. For herself. For Xavier. Because maybe this was more than just chemistry with an expiry date…

She took a deep breath. 'I want to apologise. For something I said to you on our first evening together.'

He'd gone still, but she sensed it wasn't an angry stillness.

'Go on,' he prompted.

She hugged her knees, swivelled round to face him. 'I asked you if you would love your children as—as if there was a possibility you wouldn't,' she said quietly. 'It was a terrible thing to imply, and I'm sorry. Yesterday, seeing you with your parents… Well, I could see how much you love and respect them, so family is obviously important to you. I imagine that when you have children you will love them very much.'

He was silent again. Jordan could hear her heartbeat in her ears.

Then he reached his hand across and circled her ankle, gently stroking his thumb over the top of her foot. 'Thank you, *querida*. But your apology is not necessary. In those first days of our acquaintance I didn't present myself in the best light. You weren't unjustified in thinking the worst of me.'

Jordan breathed deeply again. That hadn't been so hard…but this next bit might be.

'Your parents are lovely, Xavier,' she said with a soft smile. 'And they so obviously adore each other after many years of marriage.' She paused. 'I wondered why, when you have such a beautiful example of a loving marriage, you would dismiss that for yourself.'

She felt his fingers tense on her ankle, the grip almost painful, but forced herself to finish.

'Does it have anything to do with the woman you and Diego fought over?'

Xav saw her slight wince and withdrew his hand. He didn't desire to have this conversation. He had told her before he wasn't interested in the past and he meant it. But he recognised that she was looking for something from him. Something he feared he couldn't give her.

Yet he could give her other things. More important things. More valuable things.

This, perhaps, was the opening he needed. One brief, uncomfortable conversation was an acceptable sacrifice to get what he wanted. And in the past forty-eight hours it had become crystal-clear in his mind that what he wanted was Jordan.

He shifted on the lounger, creating space and holding out his arm. 'Come, *querida*.'

She hesitated, but then came to him, curling into his arms, her body soft and warm through her thin sarong.

He removed her sunglasses, resting his jaw on top of her head. 'Ten years ago I met a woman I came to believe I wanted to marry.'

Jordan was silent a long moment. When she spoke he felt the warmth of her breath on his chest.

'Because you thought you loved her?'

He drew air through his nose, exhaled it slowly from his mouth. '*Sí.* I believed she was…special.'

So 'special' he had introduced her to his family. Told his mother she was The One. Bought an expensive ring.

'Who was she?'

'A young American heiress. We met through social circles.'

'And what happened?'

'I proposed and she turned me down.'

'She didn't love you?' she asked gently.

'No.'

Jordan rose up on her elbow. 'I'm so sorry, Xavier.' Her eyes were soft with compassion. 'That must have been incredibly difficult—and painful.' She paused, biting her lip. 'But…would you deny yourself the chance to love again just because of one bad experience?'

His gut knotted with tension—and a touch of anger. A *bad* experience? It'd been the single most humiliating, soul-destroying experience of his life.

But she wouldn't understand that unless he told the whole story.

'There's more.'

He eased her head down to his shoulder again. He didn't want her watching him. Already he felt too exposed.

'She told me she would've married me in a heartbeat if I was my parents' biological son. She said there was no point marrying into aristocracy if her children wouldn't inherit the bloodline.'

Memory churned in him like acid. Natasha had dismissed their relationship as just a bit of fun. She'd even admitted that she'd allowed him to introduce her to his family in the hopes of snaring his brother.

He made a rough noise in his throat. 'She said she couldn't possibly marry someone of "unknown origin" for fear of what her children would inherit.'

'What?'

Jordan popped up again. This time she wouldn't be encouraged back down. Angry colour bloomed on her cheekbones.

She shook her head, curled her hand into a fist on his thigh. 'And where does that scumbag Diego fit in?

He tucked a flying curl behind her ear. Her furious indignation on his behalf was almost adorable. Incredibly he felt his chest lighten—enough for him to be able to admit, 'He slept with her within days of our break-up. And ensured the reason why she'd rejected me became gossip fodder in our social circles.'

'Oh, Xavier.' She touched his jaw. 'I'm so sorry.'

'It is in the past.'

'Yet it affects your life to this day.'

He shook his head. 'It doesn't.'

'How can you say that?' she persisted. 'When you won't let yourself love?'

'It is not a matter of allowing myself. I simply have no interest in it. A few people, like my parents, find it—or a version of it, at least—but others waste their lives looking for it. Or waiting for it.'

She dropped her hand. 'You think love is a waste of time?'

He shrugged. 'I don't believe love is the magic bullet many people think it is. It comes with pressure, expectation. Those things can break a relationship.'

She frowned, pulled back. Xav reined in his frustration. This wasn't the reaction he wanted.

He kept an arm around her waist. 'There are many things besides love—*good* things,' he emphasised, 'that can contribute to a successful relationship.'

'Like what?' she said, her voice croaky.

Sensing her on the edge of flight, he tightened his hold. 'Respect, friendship, affection, security...' He traced his fingertip over the swells of her breasts above the sarong and her skin flushed with goosebumps. His voice roughened. 'Desire.'

He saw her eyes flare. Saw the moment she understood. 'What are you saying?'

'You know, *querida*. We're good together. We can *have* something good together. Something lasting.'

All she had to do was see sense and give up on her silly notion of love.

Her breathing was uneven. 'You said we'd burn out… it's just chemistry—'

'I was wrong. I do not say this to be boastful, but I've had many lovers. This attraction we have…it's powerful, different… It won't burn out.'

'Xavier…' She braced her hand on his chest. 'I've received a job offer—in Sydney. I need to attend an interview in a couple of weeks—'

'It's not confirmed?'

'No, but—'

He laid a finger against her lips. 'Then you have time. Let us enjoy this next week, *si*? No pressure.'

The uncertainty on her face only intensified his resolve. There were two options here. She would either stay or walk away. The latter he couldn't countenance. This woman had affected him like no other. Hell, sitting in his desk drawer right now were résumés from the exclusive matchmaker for three beautiful, eligible women, and not one of them stirred his blood like Jordan did.

He needed to start his campaign of persuasion with a win. Demonstrate he was the kind of man she wanted to be with.

He smoothed her hair back from her face. 'Since we are having an honest conversation, I have a confession. In Madrid, when I found your journal, it was open—

and I saw something.' He paused. 'You have brought Camila's ashes to Spain, *si*?'

She blinked, and a look of such naked vulnerability came over her face he wanted to hold her against his chest and never let go.

'Would you like me to be with you when you scatter them, *querida*?'

Her mouth trembled and tears welled in her eyes. Big, fat tears that rolled down her cheeks and made his chest ache.

He brushed them away with his thumbs. 'Is that a yes?'

She curled her hands over his wrists and whispered, 'Yes.'

Jordan went into the week in a state of shellshock—and Xavier gave her no chance to recover.

On Monday he surprised her with a visit to an exclusive day spa where, for several hours, a team of beautiful therapists scrubbed and plucked and buffed her until every inch of her glowed.

On Tuesday morning they flew to London and went to the penthouse suite at one of Ramon's private clubs. In the afternoon Xavier disappeared to a meeting, leaving her in the suite with a personal stylist who arrived with a vast collection of evening gowns, a bottle of champagne and a case full of make-up and hair products. In the evening he took her to see *Les Misérables*. They had the best seats in the theatre, of course, and afterwards ate a late supper at a Michelin-starred restaurant.

But as the week progressed it wasn't the pampering, or the posh restaurants and luxury suites, or the beautiful evening gown she wore in London—or even their incredible, intense lovemaking—that made her wonder whether she could compromise. Whether she could settle for what he offered and live without ever hearing those three little words.

Rather, it was the little things that cost nothing that burrowed under her defences.

It was the look of stupefied awe on his face when he first saw her in the evening gown.

It was the almost imperceptible tremor in his hands as he helped her put on a stunning choker of diamonds and yellow sapphires and his anxious expression when he asked her if she liked it.

It was the hour they spent with Emily and Ramon at their beautiful Chelsea home before returning to Barcelona. She'd blown raspberry kisses on Katie's tummy and looked up to find Xavier watching, a smile playing about his mouth. That night, after making love, he gently kissed her stomach and said how sexy she would look when she was round with child, and what a wonderful mother she would be.

It was every shared smile, every lingering look, every moment of heart-rending tenderness.

Early in the week she attempted to broach the subject of his birth father. Now she knew about the brutal rejection he'd suffered, his reluctance to learn about his biological origins made more sense. It was fear. That awful woman had put the idea in his head that he might somehow be defective.

But he shut her down. Gently but nevertheless firmly.

On Wednesday she contacted Maria Gonzalez anyway. Asked the older woman if she'd assist her to make some discreet enquiries.

Maria was delighted to help, but she was also concerned. 'There was a man here last weekend. Asking about Camila. He said he was tracing family history, but something did not feel right. I did not know if it was important enough to call you.'

Jordan's nape prickled. 'Did you tell him anything?'

'No. Benito sent him away. Told him we did not remember her. But he spoke to other people. People who may have known Camila.'

When Xavier came home he looked unusually tired. He said he was fine but, seeing the lines of strain around his mouth, she decided it wasn't the time to mention Maria's concerns.

On Thursday night, before the sun set, they walked down to the beach and scattered Camila's ashes into the ocean. Afterwards they spread a blanket on the sand, opened a bottle of brandy—Camila's favourite tipple—and saluted her.

Xavier pulled her back against him, his arms strong, his body warm and comforting. 'Tell me about her,' he invited, and she did.

By the time they went to bed that night she'd accepted that she was hopelessly, desperately in love with this man.

And then finally, on Friday morning, it all came to a terrible, terrible end.

CHAPTER TWELVE

SHE WOKE WITH a start and a single word comprised her first thought.

Friday.

The day she had promised herself she would make her decision. The hospital in Sydney had confirmed an interview for next Thursday. She needed either to withdraw her application or change her return flight to depart Spain on Sunday.

She loved him.

The thought made her heart leap, and at the same time filled her with a bone-deep ache of desperation and despair.

He had made his position clear. Love was not on the table. Not part of what he was offering. And yet she still hoped. Still held her breath for those three tiny yet monumental words.

There was still today, she thought with an optimism she had to force with every ounce of will she possessed. She could wait and make her decision tonight.

She got up and slipped on a robe. Morning sunlight slanted through the bedroom's shutters, casting pale yellow stripes across the navy satin sheets.

Xavier had decided to work from home today. She

didn't know whether that was significant. Perhaps he, too, had mentally marked Friday as D-day. Given the sheets on his side were cold, he must have risen early, decided to let her sleep and gone to his study.

The door was ajar. She listened for a moment to ensure she wouldn't intrude on a phone call, then went in.

Xavier wasn't at his desk. He stood at the French doors to the terrace, staring out, and the instant Jordan's gaze fell on him a cold wave of anxiety washed over her.

His hands were fisted and the taut, rigid lines of his body screamed tension. Even from behind, without his expression visible, he looked like a man poised on the edge of violence.

'Xavier?'

He turned, and she gasped at what his hard-set features revealed. There was anger, even rage, but she saw bleakness, too. He stalked across the office, took her briefly in his arms, kissed her forehead, then drew her to a chair.

She stared at him, her heart racing, her mouth dry. 'Xavier, what's happened? You're frightening me.'

He picked up a computer tablet from his desk. 'Sit. I need to show you something. And it's not pleasant.'

'Okay,' she said slowly, and lowered herself into the chair, legs trembling. 'Just…just give it to me, then.'

Mouth grim, he handed over the tablet—and Jordan's horror was instantaneous.

On its own, the salacious tabloid headline was shocking—*Vega Corporation CEO Cavorts with Stepsister!*—but it was the photograph that sent mortified heat sweeping over her skin, followed by a wave of cold, prickling sweat.

Reluctantly she scrolled and—*Oh, God*—there were more photos, all taken with a powerful telephoto lens.

'This was last Friday,' she whispered.

The night they'd fooled around in the pool.

She covered her mouth with a trembling hand. She felt sick. Violated. Every photo was hideously explicit. It wasn't so bad for Xavier. A bare male torso was hardly risqué, although one shot had captured half a toned buttock. But for Jordan…

She burned with humiliation and shame. She couldn't even look up and meet Xavier's eye.

She scrolled down and read the text, but could barely absorb the words. Her mind was too shaken. Some things penetrated or jumped out. Names, for instance. Xavier's. Hers. Camila's.

Then her eye caught on another name.

Tomás Garcia.

Xavier's birth father.

Jordan doubled her efforts to focus and her grip on the tablet grew tighter, and tighter. Horror turned to outrage. 'These are lies!'

Xavier gave a grim smile. 'Regrettably, I think the photos speak for themselves, *querida*.'

'No.' She put the tablet down. Just holding it made her feel dirty. 'I mean about your father.'

His gaze hardened. 'Vittorio de la Vega is my father.'

'You know what I mean,' she said, but gently, because he had to be hurting. 'This can't be true.'

'Yet there it is in black and white,' he said flatly.

'In a *tabloid*.' She spoke more forcefully now. 'They print rubbish. Half-truths. Lies.' She stood. 'Tomás Garcia was *not* a criminal.'

His jaw flexed. 'And you know this how?'

'Because I knew Camila. I think she had strong feelings for Tomás. I don't believe she would have fallen in love with a bad man.'

His expression grew shuttered. 'Well, we'll never know now, will we? Because they're both dead.' He moved behind his desk. 'In any case, it is irrelevant.'

His coldly dismissive tone made her flinch. 'How can you say that?'

'Because my only priority right now is damage control.' He waved to where the tablet sat. 'This harms not only me but the company. We have shareholders, clients, investors, joint venture partners who will all be concerned about the negative impact of a deliberate attack on my reputation and the company's image.'

Belatedly she registered that he wore business attire. 'Who do you think is responsible?'

A vein pulsed in his temple. 'Diego and Hector.'

Jordan sat back down with a thump. 'Oh, no. I've just remembered. I was speaking with Maria Gonzalez on Wednesday. She said a stranger was in the village last weekend, asking questions about Camila.'

Xavier stilled in the act of gathering papers. 'Why were you speaking with Maria Gonzalez?'

She couldn't lie. 'I—I asked her if she would help me trace your birth father,' she confessed.

An awful stillness—the kind that said he was utterly furious—pervaded his whole body.

A terrible quietness came to his voice. 'Why, Jordan? When I specifically stated I wasn't interested?'

She swallowed. 'Because I thought it would help you.'

'Do I strike you as a man who needs your help?'

Something in his tone, in the way he said *your* help, raked painfully over her flesh.

She notched up her chin. 'No. You strike me as a man who's too proud to ask for *anyone's* help. Too proud to admit that you might not have everything perfectly under control.'

His jaw hardened. '*Gracias.* That was a most insightful assessment. Anything else you'd like to add, since you're clearly quite the expert on me?'

She blinked back the hot sting of tears. 'Yes,' she said—because why not go for broke? Her heart was already bleeding.

She pulled the edges of her robe together and stood up for added courage.

'I think you're a strong, principled, incredible man, Xavier de la Vega, but I also think you're afraid. I think you've pushed yourself towards perfection your whole life to prove you're worthy, but deep down you fear you're not. I think love scares you, but only because you're afraid to *be* loved—because you think it means constantly living up to someone's expectations. Constantly proving yourself. But guess what?' She took a breath. '*You're* the only one who puts impossible expectations on yourself. The people who love you accept you as you are.' She flicked away a tear before it fell. 'You might be able to control everything else in your life, but you can't control who loves you. And I'm sorry to say I do.'

Before he cut her down with another pithy response, she strode from the room.

Xav drove to work in the Aston Martin, barely keeping within the speed limit.

His gut churned and his blood pumped so hard he feared for his arteries.

This morning, right on cue, Hector had called an impromptu board meeting.

The bastard.

Xav wanted to wring his neck—and Diego's. Not for a second did he doubt their culpability.

He stalked into the office, barking out orders and summonses. Lucia was flustered. Whether from stress or because she now knew what her boss's butt looked like naked, he didn't care to guess.

He slammed his door shut. He had to focus. Prepare. But damn if he could get Jordan's impassioned speech out of his head. He still felt the impact of every word. It was as if she'd taken a scalpel to his chest, slicing away layers of skin and muscle and bone until only his heart remained, unprotected and defenceless.

He wanted to punish her for defying his wishes, shake her for saying things no one else dared say to him and demand she take back her declaration of love.

He also wanted to gouge out the eyes of every man on the planet who'd ogled the photos of her lush breasts in the last twelve hours.

Those breasts belonged to him.

Every damn part of her belonged to him.

He breathed deeply. He also wished he could un-see those words he'd buried in a recess of his brain, because he had no emotional capacity to deal with them right now: Tomás Garcia—his birth father—had been shot and killed thirty-three years ago while holding up a convenience store.

Within the next half-hour his brother and his parents arrived. Xav faced them with a throat thickened by a mix of humiliation, gratitude and exasperation. 'I told you, you didn't need to come.'

'And miss the fireworks?' Ramon, sharp in a three-piece suit, slapped him on the shoulder. '*Hermano*, I've waited many years to see you in the hot seat for once, instead of me.'

Xav turned to his parents, searched their faces for disappointment or disapproval and found neither.

His father, also smart in a bespoke suit, stood between his sons and gripped their shoulders, the gleam in his eye almost anticipatory. 'It's been too long since I went a few rounds with Hector. That old scoundrel doesn't know what he's in for.'

Xav felt his chest expand. He'd thought he could handle this alone, but now his family were here he was overwhelmed by the strength of his gratitude. By the strength of their unconditional love.

His mother took him aside. 'How is Jordan?'

'She's all right.'

His conscience pricked. He had no idea if that was true. He hadn't had time to chase her after she'd stalked from his study. He'd had to get himself here.

A sudden cold sweat hit between his shoulder blades. Was she at this very minute packing her bag? Preparing to run?

He fisted his hands, a silent, primal scream rising inside him. He could not lose her.

Damn this board meeting.

Damn Hector and Diego.

Lucia popped her head in. 'Everyone's here and waiting in the boardroom.'

His mother sat down. 'Good luck, *mis queridos*. I shall wait here.'

The meeting was hellish, worsened by the unexpected presence of a smirking Diego.

'He's a shareholder—and family,' Hector blustered when Ramon challenged Diego's attendance.

When the PR Director started outlining a multi-faceted strategy for mitigating the reputational risk Xav tuned out. He wanted out of there. *Needed* to be out of there. Jordan could be running right now. To an airport, a train station, a ferry terminal, a bus depot. Did he have enough people to cover every possible departure point?

Afterwards the PR guy asked Xav to hang back for a quick word. He gritted his teeth and checked his watch. 'You have one minute.'

Ramon waited in the anteroom, one shoulder propped against the wall. Across the space Diego lingered, looking at his phone.

Xav walked past without acknowledging him, then stopped abruptly and swung back. '*What* did you say?'

Diego was smug. 'I said are you rushing home to slutty sis?'

In a move thirty years overdue Xav swung his fist, his knuckles connecting with Diego's nose with a painful but savagely satisfying crunch. Diego went down on one knee, clutching his bloodied nose, his watering eyes agog.

Xav leaned down. 'You're talking about my future wife and the woman I love,' he snarled. 'So watch your mouth, *cousin*.'

On his way to the car he called Lucia. 'I'm not coming back to the office.'

'Peter Reynaud has just called. He wants to video conference this afternoon.'

'Tell him I'm not available.'

If the deal went belly-up, so be it.

* * *

Xav's heart thundered as he navigated the final stretch of winding road up to the villa.

Despair outweighed hope. Thirteen times he'd called her mobile. Thirteen times he'd got her voicemail.

He had only himself to blame. What reasons had he given her to stay? Plenty, he'd thought until today—but they were the wrong reasons. He'd tried to seduce her with a taste of the lifestyle he could provide, but Jordan couldn't be bought.

Only one thing mattered to her, and it was the one thing he'd refused to give. He'd wanted Jordan in his life, but on *his* terms. And, frankly, his terms had sucked.

He slammed to a stop in front of the villa, frowning at the blue Mercedes sedan in the courtyard.

Hope grabbed a foothold.

He strode inside and scaled the stairs two at a time. If her things were still here—

'Xavier.'

His heart stopped. He turned and she stared up at him from the bottom of the stairs. Relief surged—so powerful he gripped the iron balustrade to keep himself from swaying.

He flew back down, ready to gather her into his arms, to tell her what he needed to tell her, but she stopped him with a palm on his chest.

'There's someone here,' she said. 'Someone I've brought to meet you.'

Before he could speak she walked into the living room, leaving him no choice but to follow. Her hair was caught in a ponytail and she wore the wraparound skirt she'd worn that day he'd practically kidnapped her outside her hostel. He wanted to loosen her hair, pull the ties on her skirt—

'Xavier—' She cleared her throat. 'This is Luis Garcia. Luis is your uncle…' She paused, and her smile wobbled a bit. 'Your biological uncle.'

His gaze snapped to the man rising to his feet and a sensation he'd never experienced before punched through his chest. Luis Garcia was tall, broad-shouldered, and distinguished-looking in a suit, and as he came forward with his hand outstretched Xav, for the first time in his life, looked into the face of someone whose features were strikingly like his own.

'I'll leave you two to talk,' Jordan murmured, and retreated from the room.

Her trembling legs carried her all the way to Xavier's bedroom, where she sank onto the end of the bed. She pressed her hand to the base of her throat.

Had she done the right thing?

Only time would tell.

Tears of bittersweet joy stung her eyes. After their awful parting this morning, the look on Xavier's face when he'd seen her just now and his unmistakable eagerness to take her in his arms had sent her heart soaring. But she'd had to remind herself that his desire to make peace didn't mean anything had changed.

She drifted onto the balcony and stayed there for a long time, until eventually she saw Xavier and Luis emerge into the sunlight below.

They shook hands, and there seemed to be some kind of camaraderie between them, and then Luis drove away.

Xavier must have sensed her gaze. He turned and

looked up and their eyes locked, but she couldn't tell anything from his expression. Then he came inside and she waited for him in the bedroom, knowing he would come to her.

As soon as he walked in he folded her in his arms, and she almost sobbed it felt so good.

He spoke against her hair. 'Thank you.'

She could have stayed there for ever, tucked against his warm, strong body, but she eased away. 'He told you everything?'

He nodded, compressing his lips for a moment, as though he didn't trust himself to speak, and her heart swelled to see him so moved.

Tomás Garcia had not been a criminal. An innocent bystander, caught up in a vicious armed robbery, he'd stepped into harm's way to protect a female store worker. He had died a hero.

'He never knew Camila was pregnant,' she said. 'His parents kept them apart.'

'*Sí.*'

Their gazes fused, and she felt as if her insides were filling with molten silver.

'Stay, Jordan.'

The quiet plea catapulted her back to that first night when she'd tried to leave and he'd implored her to stay. How could so much have changed in two weeks? How could *she* have changed so much?

She opened her mouth but he surged forward, and suddenly his mouth was on hers.

For a second she stiffened, expecting his kiss to be searing and fierce, an explicit, forceful reminder of their explosive chemistry. But it was something else. Something deeply intimate and tender. Something that melted her from the inside out and made her tummy flutter with hope.

His hands framed her face, anchoring her as he raised his head.

'Xavier—'

'I love you.'

Her breath caught. 'What?'

'I love you, *querida*,' he said. 'And everything you said this morning, as difficult as it was to hear, was right. In that board meeting I was under attack—but I had people beside me who love me, who had my back and will always have my back. I could have done it without them, but I didn't need to. Because they were there, without judgment, without criticism. And through most of that meeting all I could think about was getting back here. Those photos—' His jaw clenched for a second. 'I want to be the man who protects you, the man who has your back, the man who stands by your side and accepts that he's human and imperfect.'

Tears clung to her lashes. 'I love you, too,' she whispered.

'Marry me,' he said.

She laughed. 'Is that an order?'

'*Sí.*' He lifted her left hand and stroked her fingers. 'I will buy you a magnificent ring.'

She started to say that she didn't need a big diamond, just something small, given with love, but then she gasped. 'Xavier! What happened to your knuckles?'

'I punched Diego—defending your honour.'

Her eyes widened, then she grinned. 'Did it feel good?'

'Very.' Xavier flexed his hand and grinned back. Then he tugged her towards the bed. 'But I know something that will feel even better.'

* * *

At midnight, unable to sleep, Xavier gently disentangled himself from Jordan's soft, sleep-heavy limbs, pulled on a pair of drawstring pants and went to his study.

He poured a brandy, sat at his desk and read the letter his birth mother had written to him in the weeks before she died.

When he got to the end he wiped his cheeks, put the letter away and raised his glass to Camila Walsh—the woman who had not only given him life, but given him the love of his life.

Jordan.

* * * * *

If you enjoyed
A MISTRESS, A SCANDAL, A RING
check out the first part of Angela Bissell's
RUTHLESS BILLIONAIRE BROTHERS *duet*

A NIGHT, A CONSEQUENCE, A VOW

and Angela Bissell's
IRRESISTIBLE MEDITERRANEAN
TYCOONS *duet*

SURRENDERING TO THE VENGEFUL ITALIAN
DEFYING HER BILLIONAIRE PROTECTOR

All available now!

COMING NEXT MONTH FROM

HARLEQUIN

Presents.

Available July 17, 2018

#3641 THE GREEK'S BOUGHT BRIDE
Conveniently Wed!
by Sharon Kendrick

When Tamsyn loses her innocence to Xan, she doesn't expect to see him again—until he proposes a marriage of convenience. Xan is dangerously addictive... If Tamsyn isn't careful, she could lose herself to him—for good...

#3642 WED FOR HIS SECRET HEIR
Secret Heirs of Billionaires
by Chantelle Shaw

To shake his playboy reputation, Giannis enlists beautiful Ava to pose as his fiancée. But when Giannis learns Ava is keeping the consequences of their passion a secret, to legitimize his child, he'll make Ava his wife!

#3643 SHEIKH'S BABY OF REVENGE
Bound to the Desert King
by Tara Pammi

Seeking revenge for his royal family's rejection, warrior sheikh Adir seduces his brother's innocent fiancée! But when he discovers that their illicit encounter left her pregnant, he'll claim his baby with a vow...

#3644 MARRIAGE MADE IN BLACKMAIL
Rings of Vengeance
by Michelle Smart

Luis's reputation needs restoring after a scandalous business feud. Chloe will pay for her part in it—by marrying him! Their attraction is explosive, but Luis requires more than blackmail to make Chloe his bride...

HPCNM0718RA

#3645 THE ITALIAN'S ONE-NIGHT CONSEQUENCE
One Night With Consequences
by Cathy Williams
When Leo meets Maddie, their irresistible chemistry ignites. Then Leo learns Maddie is heiress to the company he wants—and she's *pregnant*! To secure his heir, can Leo strike a deal to meet Maddie at the altar?

#3646 TYCOON'S RING OF CONVENIENCE
by Julia James
Socialite Diana's determination to save her family home provides self-made billionaire Nikos with the opportunity to propose a temporary marriage. But during their honeymoon, Nikos awakens Diana's simmering desire! Now Nikos craves more from his not-so-convenient wife...

#3647 BOUND BY THE BILLIONAIRE'S VOWS
by Clare Connelly
When Skye learns her marriage to Matteo is built on lies, she demands a divorce. But Matteo isn't willing to let Skye go so easily—the price of her freedom is one last night together!

#3648 A CINDERELLA FOR THE DESERT KING
by Kim Lawrence
When shy Abby pledges herself to a mysterious stranger, she's shocked to learn he's heir to the throne. Swept into Zain's world of exquisite pleasure, can this innocent Cinderella ever become this powerful sheikh's queen?

YOU CAN FIND MORE INFORMATION ON UPCOMING HARLEQUIN® TITLES, FREE EXCERPTS AND MORE AT WWW.HARLEQUIN.COM.

HPCNM0718RB

"You want me to move?"

"Yes."

A gleam pulsed in his eyes. "Make me."

Instead of closing her hand into a fist and aiming it at
his nose as he deserved, Chloe placed it flat on his cheek.

An unwitting sigh escaped from her lips as she drank
in the ruggedly handsome features she had dreamed
about for so long. The texture of his skin was so different
from her own, smooth but with the bristles of his stubble
breaking through…had he not shaved? She had never
seen his face anything other than clean-shaven.

He was close enough for her to catch the faint trace of
coffee and the more potent scent of his cologne.

Luis was the cause of all this chaos rampaging through
her. She hated him so much, but the feelings she'd carried
for him for all these years were still there, refusing to die,

making her doubt herself and what she'd believed to be the truth.

Her lips tingled, yearning to feel his mouth on hers again, all her senses springing to life and waving surrender flags at her.

Just kiss him...

Closing her eyes tightly, Chloe gathered all her wits about her, wriggled out from under him and sat up.

Her lungs didn't want to work properly, and she had to force air into them.

She shifted to the side, needing physical distance, suddenly terrified of what would happen if she were to brush against him or touch him in any form again.

Fighting to clear her head of the fog clouding it, she blinked rapidly and said, "Do I have your word that your feud with Benjamin ends with our marriage?"

Things had gone far enough. It was time to put an end to it.

"*Sì.* Marry me and it ends."

Don't miss
MARRIAGE MADE IN BLACKMAIL,
available August 2018,
and the first part of Michelle Smart's
RINGS OF VENGEANCE *trilogy*
BILLIONAIRE'S BRIDE FOR REVENGE,
available now wherever Harlequin Presents® books
and ebooks are sold.

www.Harlequin.com

HARLEQUIN Presents

**Coming next month, a tale of
inescapable passion!
In *THE GREEK'S BOUGHT BRIDE*
by Sharon Kendrick!**

**Tamsyn is about to get a shocking proposal from
devastating Greek billionaire Xan. But will she
accept his convenient ring?**

Tamsyn lost her innocence in a spectacularly sensual
night with a Greek billionaire. She didn't expect to see
notorious playboy Xan again, until he proposes a marriage
of convenience! It's hard to refuse when he's promising
incredible wealth and her pregnant sister desperately needs
support, but Xan is dangerously addictive… If Tamsyn isn't
careful, she could lose herself to the Greek—for good!

The Greek's Bought Bride
*part of the **Conveniently Wed!** miniseries!*

Available August 2018

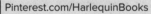